DEAD AS
DEAD AS
INKIN'DEAD
AD AND STINKIN
DEAD AND STINKIN'D
STINKIN'

STEPHEN HEWETT

DEAD AND STINKIN'

WHERE
**HIP HOP
LITERATURE**
BEGINS...

AUGUSTUS
PUBLISHING

© 2010 Augustus Publishing, Inc.
ISBN: 9780982541555

All stories by Stephen M. Hewett ©2005 Stephen M. Hewett ©2006 Stephen M. Hewett

Novel by Stephen Hewett
Foreword by Anthony Whyte
Edited by Anthony Whyte
Creative Direction &
Photography by Jason Claiborne

Augustus Publishing paperback July 2010
www.augustuspublishing.com

ACKNOWLEDGEMENTS

It's amazing how we are able to find strength in the darkest places and from the most heart aching situations. My strength, courage and inspiration to write this story and the ones to follow came from the unyielding stress of my incarceration. A portion of this dedication goes out to the people who helped nurture that stress. This goes out to the women in my life who abandoned me shortly after my incarceration. Thank you for those stressful, insensitive and sometimes cruel letters, or better yet, thanks for not writing at all. Thanks to all my associates who had long chips but chose not to put a dime in my commissary. Good looking out, goes to all those fake jokers in my life. I wholeheartedly thank you for the sorrow you caused me that eventually turned into strength for me.

Putting the last remaining bitterness aside, I would now like to thank the troopers in my life. Big up to my brother Paul, and my partner Shack, who held me down from start to finish. Excess amount of honor is due to my Mother, Aunt and beloved Grandmother who never left my side an inch.

To my children whose letters and visits kept a little warmth in an otherwise ice-cold heart, I say thank you my babies. To each and every soul who contributed, be it negatively or positively in the creation of the Author that I've become, I sincerely say, "Thanks, I couldn't have done it without your help."

Shout out to all the readers, thanks for supporting. Special thanks to the Augustus Manuscript Team, Tamiko Maldonado, Jason Claiborne, Juliet White, Anthony Whyte. The dream team, great work!

Prelude to a Tale

Many stories have been written, some with tragedy, humor or sex.

History has bought us a variety, from war and peace to Oedipus Rex.

The Author of this literary work is no well-bred Ivy League scholar;

He's just your average inner-city brother, who use to hustle for a dishonest dollar.

Everyday new books are written, about thug life, hustling and jails;

So it dawned on me one day, why not revise some classical tales.

The inspiration for these stories comes from ancient, mythological fiction.

The themes and plots are timeless, but written in our modern day diction.

I may never join the ranks with Authors like Goines, Angelou or Hughes;

But like those respected black Authors, I have certainly paid my dues.

There are messages in every chapter; I hope most will decipher my flow;

It's been written for a higher purpose, but I could definitely use the dough.

FOREWORD

ANTHONY WHYTE

God knows I'm a Voodoo Child
I didn't mean to take up all your sweet time,
I'll give it back one of these days
Song: Voodoo Chile, Jimi Hendrix

Supernatural or magic, the belief in the unknown, superstitions and folklore are like bootleg videos in the hood—every culture has one. Or you know someone who goes through daily rituals, you might consider strange, and not even understand. My mother, Violet Wade, was a Seventh Day church of God, Christian. On Saturdays she attended services religiously. She even had me going for awhile. Cooking was forbidden on Fridays after sundown until sundown Saturdays. Also prohibited was the eating of certain flesh, such as the swine and certain seafood— These foods were considered part of the devil and eating or partaking of them in any form was believe to bring Satan into your mind. Through eating these types of meats, the soul of the killed animal would penetrate through your intestines and into the mind via the body. Is it a superstition or real? It really doesn't because I still don't eat pork, and certain flesh. My mother went to high school in Jamaica, I'm a college grad. Superstitions is not based on education level, it is based on the culture you were raised in.

Ritual has nothing to do with one's career. I know this older Italian, a former hit man in the streets, who makes the sign of the cross twice daily and attends church weekly, periodically confessing his sins. He said his family has always attended Catholic Church. He's a gangster, go figure. Beliefs have nothing to do with age. Another friend, a young drug dealer, Spanish, and although he doesn't attend church, he makes the sign of the cross whenever he goes by a church building. His frontin' perplexed me to the point I had to ask him why. He told me that it was the way he was brought up, not to disrespect the church. A building he won't even go in…? I laughed so hard I had to get serve by some other dealer. Then he swore using the name of Jesus and kissing his Lazarus piece dangling from his neck. Dominicans…?

I know several Jamaicans who practice the secretive art of Obeah. Then of course Haiti is known for all its diverse worshiping of voodoo and there is such an incredible array of angels and talismans, it would take a whole book on the subject. Santaria is well known amongst the Taino's of Puerto Rican.

All the Afrikans walking the streets of the cities practice some form of voodoo and their culture encourages beliefs in the unknown. Same for the Irish Americans and others practicing of the art of wicker. Few can forget the great witch-hunts across America. I called these out because they are the easiest to pick on. At this time someone you know is doing some form or the other of them, and depending on the focus it could be good… Or it could be evil, like putting you in a pine box, leaving you…DEAD AND STINKIN'

Curl up under your safety blanket of courage and I bid you welcome to the tantalizing, and very strange world of this form of storytelling. Here is an eclectic collection of stories that will not only entertain but will become part of our folklore, told by Mr. Stephen Hewett.

Preface

It was once said that a man must honor his father and mother. It was also said that eventually a man must leave his father and mother, and take a wife for his own. For all intent and purposes, this is the normal order of things. But every now and then, in this case the natural order becomes the unnatural disorder.

On that rare occasion, all things that we think should be— really shouldn't be. Things that feel oh so right, in reality, can be terribly wrong. In our search for the right answers, we might just find ourselves confronted with more questions. When faced with an unnatural disorder of events, how can one get things back on track? Hell, maybe all the chaos and turmoil in a person's life was supposed to happen. Who knows...? Damn! I said too much already... Just

DEAD AND STINKIN'D

HONOR THY MOTHER AND FATHER

Chapter 01

The couple arrived at the doctor's office one hour before their appointment. They were so anxious they couldn't wait any longer. Sitting outside the waiting area, Jackie and Larry Anderson were both becoming a vast bundle of nerves.

"Girl, you better sit your butt down! You buggin' out ain't gonna get us the results any quicker," Larry said, casually eyeing his wife.

Jackie looked at her husband, sighed loudly, slowly rolled her eyes, and pursed her lips. Sucking her teeth and dismissing his comment, she stared at him and spoke.

"Listen, Larry, this is my first pregnancy, okay? Believe me when I say that I'm crazy nervous. So Larry please let me just do me. Okay…? Thank you," Jackie said, shooting daggers with her cold stare.

He wasn't expecting such a fierce response and tried to avoid staring into Jackie's angry face. Their showdown was interrupted by a nurse at the reception desk.

"The doctor will see you now," she said.

Larry rose and offered a hand to his wife. She smiled in acceptance, and with Larry's support, they both walked into the doctor's private office.

"I can't believe it, baby, we're gonna be parents," Larry said, smiling at his wife.

"Believe me when I say that I can believe it," Jackie said, feigning a smile at first.

Happiness was welling up inside her and Jackie let what she was truly feeling shine through in her smile. The loving couple was holding hands walking out of the doctor's office. Approaching their car, Larry glanced lovingly at his wife's face. From the smile on his face, Jackie could tell he was in a real happy mood.

"Jackie, why don't we celebrate? C'mon hon, we haven't been to Coney Island in years. I think we deserve a little we time together, just the three of us," Larry said, gently touching his wife's belly.

Larry smile beamed, making him look like the hands down winner in proudest dad in the world competition. Jackie stared on torn between admiration and secretly wishing that he was the one carrying the baby.

Larry and Jackie Anderson lived in Brooklyn, New York. They had been childhood sweethearts who had been married for eight years. The couple had a loving relationship and their marriage was still going strong. Larry worked part-time as a mechanic and Jackie was a homecare attendant. Between the bills and Jackie's student loans, they had to stay on a tight budget. Unfortunately their salaries didn't allow for much leisure time, but they managed to make the best of what they had been blessed with. But Coney Island could prove expensive and Jackie already felt exhausted from the doctor's visit.

"Baby, can we afford it? We need to save all we can before our little angel gets here," Jackie warned her enthusiastic husband, all the while searching her wallet.

"Don't sweat that. I got this. I'm taking my baby moms out tonight. Let's roll, cutie," Larry smiled, opening the passenger door for a surprised Jackie.

Getting in the car, she was glowing and planted a soft kiss on her husband's cheek. She delivered a kiss so sweet it was like the very first time their lips ever meet.

"What's that for, Jackie?" he sighed.

"Just because I love you, Larry… And for giving me the best gift anyone could ever give me," she smiled, rubbing her protruding stomach.

On this warm August afternoon, Coney Island was jam

packed with revelers and tourists. School was about to reopen in two weeks, and the kids were going in for their last swing of summertime fun. Jackie and Larry walked along the boardwalk. The couple was in high spirits, and totally engulfed in each other while enjoying their blessing. Despite her reluctance at first, Jackie relaxed and was having fun laughing and singing. The fun rides at this popular summer haunt brought back childhood memories.

Screaming loudly, they rode the Cyclone Rollercoaster and the Wonder wheel. Hugging and smooching like young kids, they wandered through the Aquarium and Museum. Larry hugged his wife like a schoolboy on a hot date. Then the loving couple played a bunch of games of Chance. It shaped up to be a wonderful evening to be in the park. Jackie smiled and returned her husband's kiss with fervor. It was her way of thanking him for another beautiful idea. Larry won a few stuffed animals for his unborn baby and her, Jackie laughed and cheered. The happiest couple in Coney Island shared two Nathan's world's famous hot dogs for dinner.

"Make mine with a lot of relish," Jackie smiled.

"Here, baby, be careful, they're kind a hot," Larry said, handing Jackie her hotdog.

The couple was walking along the boardwalk, when Jackie suddenly shouted, "Larry did you just split that pole?"

Larry looked back quickly before saying, "Oh snap! I must be buggin'. My bad…"

He ran back and walked thrice around the pole he just

split. The couple were deathly superstitious. Their obsession was something they both knew they had in common since high school.

On their way to the exit that led to the parking lot, Larry and Jackie passed a booth with a man dressed peculiarly in a long red robe with gold letters standing in front of it. The sign on the booth read, *Tarot card readings and fortune telling*. The old man smiled at the couple.

"Have your palms read, my friends. Or perhaps, consult the cards to discover your destiny, learn of your future."

"Oh, baby, let's do it. I haven't had a reading in months," Jackie said with anxiety. "Let's find out about our baby. Come on, boo, let's go inside," Jackie said, grabbing Larry's hand, and practically dragging him into the booth.

"Welcome my children. Please be seated," the old soothsayer instructed. "Hold out your hand my child."

Jackie extended one hand, and held up Larry's with the other. The soothsayer looked at Jackie's palm. His expression seemed to change the more he stared. When they saw the wrinkled brow of the fortuneteller, Jackie and Larry looked quizzically at each other.

"Is something wrong, sir?" Larry asked.

The fortuneteller jumped up from his perch on hearing Larry's voice, and quickly let Jackie's hand fall.

"I, I, um, I, I saw something in your lifeline that—"

The couple stared in anticipation as the fortuneteller stopped short. He then picked up the tarot cards and held them out toward Larry.

"My son, I need you to pick a card from this deck to understand more clearly the spiritual message I received from your wife."

Larry looked scared when he glanced at Jackie. She was nervously looking back at him. Jackie nudged him.

"Larry, please," she offered. "Do it so we can leave. Believe me when I say that I feel funny about this all of a sudden."

Larry stared inquisitively at the man for a moment. Then thoughtfully pulled a card from the deck and slowly placed it face up on the table. The fortuneteller inspected the card for a few anxious moments. His eyes narrowed then widened as if he had seen something horrible.

"What is it sir, what's wrong?" Jackie asked with angst while squeezing her husband's hand, all the time keeping her fingers cross.

Looking at Jackie then Larry, the tarot reader had a shock expression clouding his face. He didn't try to hide the discomfort with what his vision was about. Shaking his head from side to side, he spoke.

"I'm so sorry my children," he said, waiting for their complete attention. "The message and signs I have received tell of a horrible future."

"Tell us what the reading said, please, sir. Whatever it is, please just tell us," Jackie said, nearing tears.

The fortuneteller walked over to Jackie and placed his hand on her stomach. Reluctantly the man dragged out his words.

"Your child, um your child," he said, pausing briefly to wipe the sweat off his forehead before continuing to speak. "I saw the accursed fate of your unborn seed."

In a flash Larry jumped up, pushed the man's hand off of Jackie's belly and screamed at him.

"What the fuck you mean…? Horrible future and accursed fate…? Whut tha…! What have you seen?"

"Larry, please let him finish. Sir, what have you seen in our future? Tell us please," Jackie pleaded.

Larry calmed down after seeing his wife was showing enough strength for the both of them.

"My child, the readings tell the same tale," the man said, before pausing for a second to look at Larry and his surprise pregnant wife. "You shall have a son," he continued. "But what should be a blessed event has been damned by an unknown curse."

Jackie stood up suddenly, and asked, "Curse! How and why?"

The teller of their misfortunes looked away before he spoke. There was a brief pause. The fortuneteller allowed the couple time to rethink their actions before he spoke.

"My child, your unborn son will be the death of a family member, and the abomination will continue. He will become sexually involved with yet another of the same bloodline."

Jackie looked on in horror as the fortuneteller's words both confused and terrified her all at once. She shook uncontrollably and did not even feel Larry's embrace.

"I'm sorry, my children. You seem like such a nice couple. I truly wish I was not the bearer of this accused prophecy, but I'm only the messenger. I will pray for you both," the fortuneteller said, doing his best to comfort the couple.

Without saying anything further, the fortuneteller got up, walked to a room in the back, and closed the curtain. Larry and Jackie were left sitting speechless for a moment. Wide eyed, they just stared at each other.

It got so silent that Larry and Jackie could hear their hearts pounding inside their chest. Staring nervously into each other's eyes, Larry and Jackie could read each other's thoughts. What started out as a wonderful day and a lovely evening by sundown had turned into a nightmare. In the last few minutes their whole life had been turned upside down and shattered. The couple walked away from Coney Island that night, their hopes and dreams of a joyous and prosperous life dashed on the side of the boardwalk at Coney Island. Silently Larry drove home while Jackie repeatedly whispered the Lord's Prayer.

Chapter 02

"Honey, I just don't see that we have a choice in this matter. Believe me when I say, I know this is murder but we can't let this baby come into the world knowing what we know."

Larry and Jackie had endless discussions about what the psychic reader told them. They had eventually decided on what had to be done. Larry still had to reassure Jackie that the abortion was necessary. They had talked about several options, and even went to three other psychics that Jackie knew and trusted. With minor differences, all the predictions were very similar. The common theme of an unborn son that would cause tragedy to the family resounded in all the psychics' predictions.

On the fateful day, Jackie sat in the abortion clinic looking at the young women and pregnant teens about to destroy their babies. Jackie began to weep. Even though her mind was made up, she still mourned her unborn seed. Larry, sitting next to his wife, noticed a short plump lady walking around. She was handing out pamphlets, and talking to some of the young expectant mothers waiting their turn. The abortion clinic was more like a little shop of horrors for both Larry and Jackie. The plump lady spotted Jackie crying, and walked over.

"This is not the only answer young lady. There are other options, you know."

Jackie looked up at the lady standing over her and Larry did the same, but with a suspicious face.

"Excuse me, miss, but what are you talking about?" Jackie asked.

The woman sat down next to the couple, handed a booklet to Larry and spoke quietly with Jackie.

"Miss, if you truly want to terminate your pregnancy, you should consider giving another couple a chance at parenthood. There are many loving couples who are unable to conceive children on their own."

The woman waited for Jackie to respond, but getting none proceeded with her spiel.

"My name is Miss Jones. I work for an organization that's desperately seeking unwanted children for adoption, and placing them with good, caring and stable families. The baby and parents, original and adopters are given a chance at a full, satisfied life. It's a win-win situation for all, and we also offer post- natal care free of charge," the woman said.

Jackie stared at the lady. She saw the sincerity in her eyes, and heard the compassion in her voice. Jackie then looked at her husband.

Seeing that she was considering what the lady was offering Larry quickly said, "Hold on, baby, don't forget about—" Larry thoughts stirred and he abruptly stop speaking. He was reminded that they were not alone by the look in his wife's eyes. He glanced at the woman and said, "Pardon me, Miss Jones, could you please give us a minute alone."

"Why yes, sir, of course. This is a decision for the both of you to make. Please take all the time you need," Miss Jones said, walking off to talk with a young girl who had just walked into the clinic.

"Jackie, are you considering this? Baby, what about the predictions?" Larry asked. Suddenly he stopped when he saw the pain on his wife's face.

Jackie stared at her husband before saying, "Baby, this is our child. I can't kill it no matter what those cards say. Believe me when I say that I know we can't take the risk of bringing that curse into our lives. Maybe if our child was raised by another family that would prevent the curse from happening," Jackie said. Cutting Larry off before he could speak, Jackie continued. "Larry, let's give our son a chance at life. Please, baby, for me."

The moment he looked into his wife's sad eyes, Larry's heart melted. He loved her so much and denying her anything was next to impossible. Larry shook his head.

"Jackie, it's your body and our baby. I can't force you to do anything that would hurt you physically or emotionally. So if you decide against the abortion it's cool with me. I just hope and pray..."

Larry's words were muffled when Jackie threw her arms around him and kissed him. Miss Jones witnessed this and came over with a smile.

"Um well, whatever you two decided it looks like someone is very satisfied with the decision."

Jackie broke off the embrace and addressed her.

"Yes, Miss Jones, we will agree to the adoption for our baby's sake. But I have one condition," Jackie said.

"Condition... Ah what condition is that?" Miss Jones asked, looking puzzled.

"I would like to see my baby one time before he is taken from me. I want to hold him and kiss him, and tell him that I'm sorry."

Miss Jones looked at Jackie then Larry before saying, "I'm sorry but that's just not our policy. We really can't allow that."

"Okay, believe me when I say that I guess there's nothing further to talk about. Have a nice day, Miss Jones," Jackie said, staring at Miss Jones.

She stood and walked over to the receptionist's desk.

"How much longer will it be?" Jackie asked the nurse.

"You're next," the nurse said.

Jackie waved at Larry and started walking toward the small operating room. Miss Jones followed her and caught up with her from behind.

"Wait, dear, maybe I can try to work something out. Please don't go in there just yet. Let's see what I can do first," Miss Jones pleaded, holding Jackie's arm.

During her pregnancy, Jackie cared for herself as if she would keep the seed developing inside her. She religiously kept her prenatal medical appointments, ate the right meals and slept right. Larry was detached and tried not to go back against the plan. He rarely talked about the son who should have brought them closer, but instead pushed them further away from each other.

The deep divide burned inside both of them, ripping the walls of tolerance they had for each other. Larry coped by being silent about it, going about his business in as usual as he could do it. Jackie bore the brunt of the burden. The pregnancy took its toll on her body and emotionally she was detached.

When the day came and she was going through labor, he drove her to the hospital and stood around anxiously waiting for the baby's arrival. It was an easy labor and Jackie went through it with no complications. Later she was thrilled while resting up in the recovery room. A nurse brought the newborn bundled in white linen.

"Oh my God, Larry, look at him! Believe me when I say he looks just like you. Poor child," Jackie said, teasing Larry.

Jackie held her seven pounds, four ounces son for the first and possibly last time. Larry looked at his son smiling. He thought of the fortuneteller's prophecy and his joy was quickly extinguished. Larry walked to the window in the recovery room and stared outside. Jackie could see his face. She knew his sorrowful thoughts, but was wrapped up with the baby in her arms. She planted gentle kisses on her son's forehead and couldn't help but to examine him from head to toe. With all his fingers and toes, her son was a healthy baby boy.

She kept on scrutinizing her baby, making sure everything was where it was supposed to be.

"This is such a cute butterfly looking birthmark behind his left ear," Jackie smiled, turning to look briefly at Larry before gushing. "He's so adorable, if only we could keep him, huh Larry?"

Miss Jones heard the tone of the mother's voice and hurriedly made her way over to Jackie's bed. She had been previously sitting in a corner of the room, but didn't like what she was hearing.

"I'm sorry, Jackie, but the longer he stays with you the harder it will be for you to let him go. So I better take him now, dear."

Jackie looked at Miss Jones as if coming out of a trance. Then she glanced up at Larry, who was still looking out the window.

"Larry, don't you want to say goodbye to your son?" Jackie asked.

Larry turned, looked at his wife and newborn then walked out the room without speaking. Jackie kissed her son for the last time and handed him over to Miss Jones. She reclined in the hospital bed and cried herself to sleep.

Days later in the office of an adoption agency in Brooklyn, prospective parents Mr. and Mrs. Wingate sat filling out papers and finally signed their names to the adoption forms. The baby born to Larry and Jackie officially changed family.

"Well, Mr. and Mrs. Wingate, all the forms have been processed and the adoption has been approved."

Paul and Mary Wingate had been waiting for this day for three years. Ever since Mary found out that she could not conceive on her own, the couple finally realized their desire. It was truly a dream come true. The Wingates, a very well to do, African American couple, were college grads, and owned a chain of dry cleaning business. They lived in midtown Manhattan in a luxurious five-bedroom apartment overlooking the East River. With future secure, their life was exciting and the only thing missing from was a child of their own. Mary Wingate shed tears of joy when news of the approved adoption hit. She hugged her husband and expressed hearty gratitude to Miss Jones.

Everything was prepared for his arrival when the Wingates brought their young handsome son home. A fully furnished bedroom awaited him and a nanny had been already screened and hired. A plan from nursery to college was already in effect. Every area of his life was already mapped out after being carefully thought out and researched. This would be the couple's only child and nothing was left up to chance. They name their son Edward, after his grandfather who had recently passed away. Even though his destiny was already decided, Edward would have the best of everything. His proud, new parents had the resources to make it happen. Unfortunately all the money and love in the world could not change one crucial area of the young Edward's life.

Chapter 03

Edward Wingate grew up to be an intelligent and handsome young man. The years went by quickly and he had already attended and graduated from a very prestigious grade school in Manhattan. An extremely good student with excellent grades, Edward, a promising athlete was scheduled to attend a preparatory high school in the fall.

"Edward, do you have everything you need?" Mary Wingate asked her son.

It was his first day of high school and she was more nervous than he was. Edward smiled at her and calmly responded.

"Yes, mother. I'm all set. I'm going to meet Chip and Roger downstairs so we can walk to school together."

With much enthusiasm and excitement, Edward kissed his mother before rushing off. However his first day at his new school started alright, but ended in unnecessary drama. After his last class ended, Edward was walking to the bus stop on his way home when he was surprised by some of his classmates.

"What's up pretty boy? Yo, you know you look like a girl," one of the boys laughed, confronting Edward.

Edward had soft facial features, but what most boys hated about him, the girls loved. He was sexually active since junior high, and was a hit with the girls on his first day in high school.

"You hear me talking to you Wingate? You look like a little bitch."

Edward ignored the boys and looked down the street for the bus. The boy doing the heckling finally worked up enough courage to get front and center in Edward's face. Before the heckling teen knew what had happened, he was flat on his back with a busted lip and a tooth missing. His friends took off leaving their pal on the floor bleeding. Edward nonchalantly stepped over the boy and walked away. This same type of fisticuffs drama had plagued Edward through grade, and now was about to do the same in high school.

After the incident with the glass jaw boy, Edward really had no more trouble with bullies in school. His peers, having quickly found out that he was no punk, respected his knuckle game. At third period, Edward was very excited because it was time for science class.

The teacher, Miss Branch, was young and fine. All the boys in school lusted and fantasized about having sex with her. Edward was much too cool to act overly excited about his teacher around his classmates, but like the rest, he constantly thought about her. Before class started, Edward was approached by one of his girlfriends.

"Eddie, I was hoping I'd catch you before class, baby."

Camille was a young Jamaican girl who was crazy about Edward. She kissed him on the cheek.

"Hey, cutie, what's up?" Edward replied, hugging Camille.

"I just wanted to give you the money for your sneaks and invite you to lunch. Are you free later?"

"But of course, Camille. How could I turn down a date with you, boo?" Edward smiled, showing off his well-cared for teeth.

Camille's eyes widened. All the girls in the school sweated Edward. Constantly angling for a better position on his list of girlfriends, they would shower him with gifts, money, and of course, sex. Edward Wingate was a fat cat in this preppy school arena. The bell rang for class and Edward kissed Camille on the cheek. He also took a hundred dollars off her.

"See you at lunch, boo," Camille shouted, walking down the hall.

She was hoping that her rivals saw Edward's affection on display toward her. Edward's friends had informed him that the science teacher, Miss Branch, always stared at him during class.

Some were jealous because she would constantly praise his work. Today the science class was about to end and Miss Branch walked to Edward's desk.

"Mr. Wingate, please remain after class. I would like to discuss your homework assignment."

The class ended and Edward waited at his desk for Miss Branch. She called him into the lab room at the back of the class. Edward walked to the dark lab room and reached for the light switch.

"Over here, Mr. Wingate."

Although Edward could barely see his teacher he walked to where Miss Branch's voice came from. Her hand grabbed his.

"What's up with the lights, Miss Branch?"

"We don't need the lights for this science project, Mr. Wingate."

Edward was a confused until the teacher took his hand and placed it between her thighs. He caught on fast.

"Miss Branch, I don't..."

He stopped speaking when the teacher started to remove her panties and rub his hands over her soft mound. Miss Branch moved closer to Edward, putting her lips inches from his ear.

"I want to see if you understand your homework assignment. It calls for you to study the female reproductive system, Mr. Wingate. Let's see what you've learned. Fuck me."

Edward wasn't new to sex. Even though he was feeling

nervous, he quickly got into position. Bending her over a desk, Edward penetrated Miss Branch. The horny teacher moaned, calling his name. Edward proceeded to blow her back out. His pounding strokes cause Miss Branch to cry out loudly and she tugged at his hair while having an extremely violent orgasm. Their fuck session seemed to last for a long time. Edward was about to discharge in his teacher for the third time when the lights suddenly came on.

"I'm sorry, Mr. and Mrs. Wingate. I'm afraid we have no choice but to expel Master Wingate from the Academy. The type of behavior he was engaged in has never happened here before, and cannot go unpunished. Miss Branch has resigned, and I called you here to discuss the board's decision."

Miss Lewis, the school principal, called the meeting with the Wingates only as a courtesy. Edward's fate had long been decided.

"Please, Mrs. Lewis, is there anything you can do to give Edward another chance? He is truly sorry for what he did. Is there anything you can do?"

Mary Wingate looked over at her son who was glancing aimlessly out the office window. She sensed that Edward had no remorse and was unaffected by the possibility of his expulsion from school. His indifference was also seen by Miss Lewis. She made her final decision.

"I'm sorry, Mr. and Mrs. Wingate, and I'm sorry Edward, but the board's decision is final. You will have to find a new school to attend. I'm truly sorry this situation had to happen."

"Let me stay, please. I don't want to go," Edward shouted out in his sleep.

The familiar cries awoke his parents. His father hurried into Edward's room, and sat on his bed.

"No, please, let me stay," Edward screamed, before his father managed to wake him.

"Edward it's me your dad. I'm here, Edward. You were just having another nightmare. It's okay, son."

Edward woke up shivering in a cold sweat. He sat up in his bed.

"Dad, why do I have the same weird dream all the while? And it always seems so real."

Since the fourth grade, Edward had been having nightmares. Usually they were all the same. He was always being taken somewhere he didn't want to go. The weirdest part about the dreams was that he could never see the faces of the people in his dreams. Tonight there was no different, but he knew they were coming more frequent. After he calmed down, Edward went into the bathroom to brush his teeth. Later his mother came into his room.

"Edward, remember we have an appointment seven thirty this morning at Dwight High School. Are you getting ready, son?"

Edward walked out of the bathroom and stared at his mother for a moment before responding.

"Ma, I'm not going back to school," he said in a decisive tone.

His arms were defiantly folded across his chest. His mother stared at him and felt sympathy.

Chapter 04

Six months passed since Edward was expelled from high school. His parents decided that the expulsion and the teacher had left him traumatized. They figured they would give him some time to get re-focused before enrolling him back into school.

Edward had no intention of returning back to school however. He started hanging around the park on Madison Avenue and smoking weed with some of the resident dealers. Edward's parents still gave him a sizeable allowance, so scoring weed and enjoying the New York City streets became a full time hobby. Edward started growing dreadlocks shortly after his pot smoking began. The new look made him even more ruggedly handsome.

One afternoon as he walked down east 27th Street on his way to the park, a very tall, black and big-butt hooker called out to him.

"Damn! You one fine brother… I think I could just fuck you for free!"

Edward glanced in her direction, wondering if she was talking to him. The hooker seductively sashayed over to where Edward stood waiting for the light to change. She put on her most fuck-me expression, before she asked, "Honey, you going out?"

"Going out where, ma'am?" Edward asked, looking at her strangely.

"Damn! You fine and innocent too… I'm cookie, and boy oh boy, I'd love to take you home and train you just right," the hooker laughed, grabbing Edward's hand.

Suddenly out of nowhere came a smooth, masculine voice.

"How'd you like to be run over by a muthafuckin' train, bitch? Get your skyscraper ass back on the track before I stomp a mud-hole in that ass!"

The threatening remarks came from a tall, light-skinned, well-dressed man walking toward Edward. When the prostitute saw him coming she almost pissed on herself and immediately started to cop a plea.

"No! Daddy, please don't. Pretty Ricky, can't you see…? I was only asking dude for a date, I wasn't—"

The well dressed man hauled off and slapped Cookie, cutting off her words. The assault came hard and swift and left the scantily clad woman sprawled on the floor. Ricky reached down and assisted his property to her feet. The pimp gently dusted her off and gave her a kiss on the cheek.

"Now get back to work, sexy, before I get mad," he said, slapping her ass.

Cookie blushed at her pimp's apparent show of affection. Quickly forgetting how she got on the ground,. This was all part of the pimp game.

"Ok, daddy, I'm gone. I'll see you later."

Before going back on the ho' stroll, Cookie reach down in her panties and pulled out a plastic bag filled with money and handed it to Ricky.

"Here's some trap money, daddy. Lemme go make you rich. Later baby," Cookie said, skipping into the streets like she was happiest woman in the world.

"Pimp hard, baby. Pimp hard," Pretty Ricky said.

"What up, pimpin'?" someone shouted.

"What's good, Silky," Pretty Ricky said to a nattily dressed man.

He appeared out of nowhere and witnessed the show. From the hugs and laughs between them, Silky was obviously one of Ricky's peers. He was a veteran midtown pimp. They both slapped each other five then looked at Edward.

"Hey, young player, I heard what my bitch said to you. It seems like she wanted to choose you, baby," Pretty Ricky said and the two pimps laughed.

"Choose me for what, sir? I don't understand…"

The men expressed their amusement, loudly laughing before directing their attention back to Edward.

"Young player, my name is Ricky and this my man Silky. What's your name?"

"It's Edward Wingate, sir."

The men again started to laugh at Edward's politeness, but quickly they got serious again. Silky spoke, "Edward Wingate, huh? It appears you have a gift with women. An old-time player once told me, if you ever find a young stud with the gift, it's your obligation to school him to the science of Pimpology. I mean we think you have the gift. So, what's up, baby boy, you down to enroll in the midtown academy of Pimpology?"

Edward stared dumbfounded at the two handsome, well-dressed men. He admired the jewelry adorning their necks, wrists and fingers. His mind was busy thinking about what the men were offering him. A young girl came out of a car that pulled up next to the curb. Looking no more than sixteen, she jumped out of the front seat, adjusting her mini skirt.

"Hey, daddy, damn you hard to find," the girl said, walking up to Silky.

She caught sight of Edward and a smile creased her lips from ear to ear. Catching herself, she handed Silky a roll of bills and kissed him on the cheek. Silky immediately started counting the money.

"Daddy, I was wondering if I could come off the track early tonight. My period just came down, and I'm having some killer cramps. Plus ain't nobody trying to buy no bloody pussy," the young girl said, smiling at her attempt at humor.

She noticed the serious screw on Silky's face and that changed her look right away. Silky brushed off his silk shirt and looked coldly into the young girl's eyes.

"Leave the track! Bitch, I ain't hear no roosters crowing, and don't give me that lame ass excuse about your bloody ass cup. As far as I can see your mouth ain't bleeding. But if you want we can change that right quick," Silky said, walking closer to his worker.

"No, daddy, no it's cool. I'll be sucking tonight 'til I get lockjaw. Don't hit me, daddy. Everything's cool."

She ran across the street to continue getting Silky's money right. All the while she kept looking back at Edward.

Edward was smiling from ear to ear. He was fascinated by what he'd seen of the life. In ten minutes, everything became clear to him. It was like an epiphany and now he knew what he was going to do with his life. Edward Wingate wanted to become a pimp.

The next couple of weeks Edward practically lived on the whore stroll between 26th and 27th streets. Pretty Ricky and Silky took him under their wings and taught him the game. Edward caught on fast, and the women were in love with the swagger of the new kid on the block.

Edward met dozens of women with legitimate jobs by

hanging on the strip and in the park. He had sex with some of them and they enjoyed spending their money on Edward. They bought him clothes and lots of expensive gifts, but none sold their body for him. He was still not a practicing pimp yet. His mentors often teased him about him getting lunch money from these squares and constantly reminded him that, "There was no better money than ho' money." Rick and Silky would enjoy flashing their fat knots of cash in his face while laughing at him.

One night, Edward arrived early on the stroll. He decided to swing by the park and score some weed then meet up with his mentors. He walked through the park but didn't see his regular dealer, Jamaican Steve. Edward was about to leave when he saw a familiar face.

"Miss Branch is that you?"

Edward's ex-science teacher looked up and smiled on seeing her favorite ex-student.

"What's up, Edward? Damn you look good. What have you been up to?"

"I'm just doing my thing, Miss Branch. What have you been doing with yourself?"

Miss Branch stood up and hugged Edward then she spoke, "Well, after I got fired, I've been looking for work ever since. The Department of Education has me on their black list. I can't get a job teaching anywhere."

Bells instantly went off in Edward's head. He smiled at the

very beautiful woman. Her hair dyed blond and her soft brown eyes greeted him.

"If you're not doing anything right now… How about we getting something to eat and talking?"

Miss Branch looked at Edward suspiciously and asked, "Talk about what, cutie?"

Edward gave her his award-winning smile before saying, "Talk about gainful employment and building your assets with those assets. Let's roll, baby doll."

Miss Branch took to prostitution like spider to a web. She was born to fuck for that paper. In a New York minute, Edward Wingate was transformed to Ed Lover, junior pimp.

Ed's new moneymaker turned out to be not only a freak, who couldn't get enough dick, she also loved to eat pussy. Before he knew it, Miss Branch's experienced tongue acquired Ed three new thoroughbred for his whores' stable. In a matter of weeks, Ed Lover became one of the hottest Macks on the circuit. His success brought on jealousy. His Pimpology instructors started noticing their trap money getting lighter and attributed this to their student's sudden rise.

"This little nigga really think he's the fucking man, Silky."

"Word, I've been checking out his movements. This cat's on a real paper chase."

Strutting down Madison Avenue, Ricky and Silky were discussing their endangered monetary units.

"Listen, baby boy, one thing for certain and two things for sure—when my money gets funny and my change gets strange, big poppa gets emotional. I think it's time young blood gets demoted real decent like," Ricky said.

"Indeed," Silky smiled, while co-signing Ricky's thoughts.

The two pimps walked upstairs to one of the hotel rooms they used as a hangout while their ladies were hard at work. Edward was already there sipping lemonade while smoking marijuana. Ricky handed a small package to Edward.

"What's this, baby," Ed Lover asked Ricky.

Ricky looked at Silky then he glanced back at Edward who was examining the small package.

"Cocaine, young stud… All the players get mellow from time to time," Ricky answered and showed Edward a dollar bill filled with powdered coke.

He gave Silky a straw and the veteran pimp took a hit. Inhaling the white powder, the pimp eased his head back and sighed.

"Your turn Lover," he said, handing the straw to Edward.

Ed Lover looked at the bill then at his mentors. He hesitated momentarily, but took the bill. He did not want to act like a square in front of these two men who he looked up to. Ed took his first hit of cocaine, and he loved it. The plan worked just as Ricky and Silky hoped it would. In less than two weeks, they had Ed Lover sniffing coke day and night.

"Baby, you got to get your shit together," Miss Branch said.

She was now known as Princess. The former schoolteacher, turned bottom-ho, was up in the hotel room trying to talk some sense into her man, Ed Lover. Her former science student turned pimp had developed a studious addiction to cocaine. It rendered him totally inept at the life. The habit proved difficult to shake and made Edward a failure.

Lately Ed Lover had started to neglect his ladies, his hygiene, resulting in his grades to fall-off and spilled over to his appearance. These were areas that were most crucial to his aura. Ed Lover's lack of efforts was becoming detrimental to his earning potential. He was doing nothing to ensure his survival. After losing four girls out of his stable, Ed Lover started seeing that he was not in control.

Two of them chose to roll with Silky and two others were busted. They were released and ran back to their small country towns. His world was falling down around him.

"You just up in this room sniffing that shit!" Princess angrily shouted.

The high walls of cocaine haze prevented Ed Lover from seeing her or hear what Princess was doing in a last ditch attempt at saving him. It was difficult for him to give up snorting. She stayed by his side, and tried to keep his declining business afloat. Even a dedicated, well-trained bottom ho' needed the education, re-education and constant instructions from her pimp.

"I can't keep making excuses for you, Ed. These bitches need to see their daddy dressing up and on point. They need to know you're still emotionally strong and on top of your pimp game. Otherwise I'm afraid all these other pimps out there with game will pull them all away from you, Ed."

Chapte 05

"Bitch, is this all the money you made last night?" Ed Lover raised his hand to reprimand his one and only whore, but decided against it.

Ever since Ed Lover, formerly Edward Wingate, had been strung out on powder cocaine, his stable of women workers had been downsized to one aging, lazy and nearly toothless employee. Princess was still his bottom ho and tried to keep Ed's business intact, but his love for cocaine outweighed his love for the game. Eventually she too went freelance on him. Seated in a raggedy hotel room in midtown Manhattan, Ed Lover counted his dwindling bankroll.

"Two hundred dollars, that's all you made for an entire night on the track?" Ed said, scolding his worker.

"I'm sorry, daddy, but tricks for some unknown reason weren't coming through tonight. It was crazy hot out there," his ho' replied.

Ed Lover watched his sole surviving whore getting busy, trying to cuddle up in bed next to him.

"Bitch what you doing? Go wash your ass before you get in this bed. You done fucked all night and sucked a bunch of dicks. Go neutralize that funk."

His final ho' looked at her decaying pimp with disgust all over her face. Ed Lover was turning into a real disgrace, and she started hatching her plan to leave him like the rest.

Coco came out of the shower and she crawled into bed with Ed. Wanting loving from her pimp, she snuggled next to him. Unluckily for her, Ed had been sniffing coke all night and his sex drive had diminished. Disgusted, she rolled over and closed her eyes.

The following night was Friday and the track was jumping. Ed dragged himself out of the hotel and limped to the stroll in order to see what was what. Most of his colleagues were out in furs, minks, flossing jewelry and getting their Mack on.

They all seemed to be staring at Ed and snickering at his raggedy appearance. Ed saw how Princess and the rest of his rouge ex-workers were running up to cars. They were hustling hard for other pimps. After locating his only source of income and giving her a five a.m. curfew, Ed went back to his room and his habit. About seven in the morning, Ed lover was awakened by a knocking on the door.

"Bitch, where's your key?" he shouted at the door.

Angrily Edward got up, stomping to the door, and opening it. It wasn't his ho at the door. To Ed's surprise it was Princess standing outside his door. Even though she had deserted his stable, he smiled when he saw her.

"Hey, Princess, what a pleasant surprise this is. Please enter, Miss Branch," he gladly welcomed.

She entered the dirty, foul-smelling room, and a frown immediately appeared.

"I'm not staying, Ed. I just wanted to pull your coat to that grimy, scandalous bitch you got. She picked a trick's pocket, and scored almost five grand from him. She was supposed to bring that trap money straight up here to you. But I can see she didn't. Ed, I'm telling you, you better find that ho before she spends all your dough."

Miss Branch looked at Ed to see his response to her news. She saw evil in his eyes. He didn't say a word, Ed threw on his worn out fox fur coat, and walked out the room. He searched for days but came up empty. Every time he went by one of the ho's hangouts, he would just missed her.

Everyone he spoke to told him she was spending money like there was no tomorrow. Finally, he ran into her on 47th Street. She was coming out of a jewelry store admiring a diamond ring she just bought. She was into her new purchase, and didn't notice her pimp walking toward her. When she looked up and saw Ed she damn near pissed her drawers.

"Hey, Lover, I was just—"

The words got stuck as Ed lover's punch sent her flying into an alleyway used for garbage disposal. She tried to get up but staggered back from the blow.

"Baby, wait a minute let me explain," she screamed.

Ed was out of his mind with rage, and got carried away with the punishment. For about five minutes, Ed punched, kicked and stomped Coco in and out of consciousness. When he finished the assault, she was almost unrecognizable.

Ed beat his only ho so badly not because she ran off with his money, whores run off every day. Most people believe Ed was really angry and frustrated with himself for letting an addiction ruin his livelihood. He just took it out on the next available person. Ed Lover's problem with his addiction was not his only concern.

A crowd gathered at the entrance to the alley. On seeing the condition the victim was in, a passerby ran to get a police officer. Ed was arrested for first degree assault and held without bail. He was taken to Rikers Island where he conferred with his court appointed lawyer.

"Three years, I have to do three years for beating up my property," Ed fumed at his Jewish mouthpiece.

"Mr. Wingate, you beat Miss Sanders to a pulp, and she is pressing charges. There are dozens of witnesses that will testify they were present during the assault. Please, sir when you go to court, don't refer to Miss Sanders as your property, for your own good."

Ed Lover's hand was forced, either cop out to three years, or face ten years if he went to trial and blew. Ed made a decision.

At Downstate Correctional Facility, Edward received his state identification number and was issued his greens. He was classified and designated to be incarcerated at Elmira Correctional Facility in upstate New York. Ed arrived at the facility and was an instant attraction. Several inmates serving long stretches fell in love when they saw the new, handsome inmate. Ed felt eyes following him as he walked to his cell. The situation made him nervous.

The first year in the facility was rough. He was constantly involved in fights with other inmates for disrespecting him about his looks. He went to the hole and was in segregation for six weeks, on three different occasions. When Ed was released the third time, he was smelling bad and decided to take a shower before chow. He got into the shower room and heard footsteps entering the outer hall area. When he turned around, he saw three unfamiliar inmates smiling behind him.

"Fuck or fight baby! What's it gonna be?" one of the men demanded, grabbing his crotch.

The biggest of the three men approached Ed smiling and said, "Damn! I ain't fuck sumthin so pretty since my grimy-ass wife. C'mon baby, don't make this hard on yourself."

"Yeah cutie, just breakdown like a twelve gauge shotgun

and run that nice ass," another horny homo-thug said.

He blew a kiss at Ed's mug. Ed had not taken off his clothes or work boots yet, and sprang into action immediately, kicking the closest potential rapist in the balls.

"Oh fuck, I'll kill you bitch," the man groaned, sinking to the floor.

Their fearless leader had been dropped by their prey and the other two men looked at each other for strength.

"What's going on in there?"

The voice of a correction officer making his rounds caused the men to turn around. Two officers entered the shower room and saw the big man on the floor moaning. They mistakenly figured that he was a rape victim and pressed their deuces for assistance. In seconds, the shower room was swarmed with correction officers. Ed was handcuff and leg chains.

He was given six months in the hole for his part in the shower room drama, along with loss of his phone and commissary privileges. When he got out of the hole, Ed was moved to a different cell block. On arriving at his new home he let out a loud laugh. In the cell was a notorious transvestite named Peaches, wearing a pair of extra tight briefs and dancing. The transvestite saw Ed's reflection in the mirror. He stopped shaking his ass and turned around.

"Oh my God, what good did I do in my life to deserve your fine ass for a cellie?" he asked, licking his lips.

Ed got along well with Peaches. The transvestite did all the cleaning and laundry. Ed had no more trouble in Elmira after the news got around about how he dropped his would-be rapist. The notoriety it gave made him received a lot of jailhouse props. He adjusted to his new home rather quickly.

One night Ed and Peaches were in their cell playing Casino. Peaches asked Ed out of the blue, "I hear you were a pimp in the world and they called you Ed Lover, is that true?" Ed just looked at Peaches and ignored his cellmate. Peaches sighed loudly then repeated, "Ed, I'm asking you a question, were you a pimp?"

Ed put down his cards and answered, "What does it matter Peaches? Shit, okay, yeah, I was a pimp, so what?"

Peaches' eyes lit up at the confirmation. He smiled and said, "Because I choose you, Ed Lover, I want you to be my daddy."

Ed Lover calculating mind went into overdrive. He knew that transvestite prostitution was big business in most state jails. With his background in marketing flesh he could turn the whole C-block into a five tier whore stroll.

The plan went into effect with Peaches acting as his only breadwinner. Soon Peaches recruited many of the already veteran prostitutes to join Ed's stable. Ed Lover had once again set himself up as a full-fledged, 'bout-his-business pimp. During a staff meeting Ed, Peaches, and four of his workers in drag were having a discussion about health coverage.

"Cuz I can't tell who got the monster up in here, so there should be precautions and coverage is absolutely necessary," a transvestite said.

"Wingate on a visit," the voice on the intercom squawked.

Their conversation was disrupted by the incoming message. Ed was puzzled. Who in the hell was visiting him after all this time? He wondered walking in front of the guard, thinking. In his two-and-a-half years in jail this was his first visit.

He was shocked when he arrived at the visiting room. It was his parents, Paul and Mary Wingate. Ed hadn't seen his parents since the day he copped out in court. They wrote him several letters but he stopped replying a long time ago. At the table, the three of them sat down, elbow to elbow in silence. A few awkward moments went by before Mary Wingate finally broke the silence.

"Hello, son, how have you been?"

Ed looked at his parents suspiciously for a couple seconds, stalling for time while he thought of what to say. He removed his hand from the table before speaking.

"I'm cool, Ma. Just counting down these last few months… What brings you two up here, after all this time?"

Paul Wingate shifted uncomfortably in his seat then looked at his wife. She looked sad when stared back at him and Edward felt his heart shuddering. Her voice wavered when she spoke.

"Edward, we came here to tell you something. We planned on telling you years ago, but ah… I guess we just couldn't find the right way to say it."

Ed attentively sat up in his chair, putting his hands back on the table, and glanced at both of them.

"Tell me what, Ma? Dad what's this all about? Please tell me."

Tears filled his mother's eyes and rolled down her cheeks. Ed reached out and held her hand and said, "Mother, it can't be all that bad. Just drop it on... I mean just tell me what it is, please."

Mary Wingate looked into Edward's eyes and disclosed her deep secret. He wasn't sure if he was ready to hear it but Edward was attentive and scared.

"Edward, my son, your father and I adopted you when you were just an infant. We're not your biological parents. I'm sorry, dear," she cried.

Edward Wingate sat frozen for a few minutes. In a split second he had lost his identity and his parents. After the shock of the news wore off, Ed began questioning the Wingates regarding his biological parents.

"So you don't know where they are or even who?"

"We told you all we know..." Mr. Wingate's voice trailed.

Edward stared at them realizing he no longer knew who he was. The ignorance made him angry but it was no use blaming the Wingates. Mary was still crying and Paul sat solemnly. The situation was stalemate. It slowly dawned on Edward that this would be last he saw of them.

They could not give him all the answers he needed, but they had told him all they knew. After the visit Ed kissed and hugged his adopted parents for the last time. He forgave them for not telling him sooner and thanked them for loving him all those years.

Ed had read a lot of books dealing with forgiveness, letting go of disappointments, and moving on while incarcerated. This was Edward Wingate's perfect opportunity to put in practice what he had been reading. Later back in his cell Ed's head hit the pillow of his bunk. He sat up but couldn't shake the feeling. His mind couldn't stop thinking. Damn adopted!

Chapter 06

Edward Wingate got into more altercations and drama during his incarceration. His rebellious behavior brought him further hardship. He lost every minute of his earned good time, and had to serve out his entire three year sentence.

After his release Edward resided at a transitional housing facility in the northeast section of the Bronx. One of the stipulations of his parole was that he could not contact with the woman who was involved in his assault case. He had to obtain lawful employment and, because of his drug history, submit to periodic random drug testing. Thursday morning found Edward at an appointment with his parole officer, Miss Jackson.

"Good morning, Mr. Wingate. And how's everything going?"

Michele Jackson was a fairly new parole officer. She graduated from John Jay College in New York City and took the parole officer's test right after her graduation. She was a young, attractive, and educated, black law enforcement officer. Most of the parolees Edward spoke with told him she was hard on them. This was her first meeting with Edward Wingate.

"Everything's going pretty smooth. I'm gainfully employed. I'm drug free, happily single and HIV negative. It's beginning to look a lot like Christmas," Edward sang,

"That's good. I see you're in a good mood, sir. And that's a positive sign. Did you bring your pay stubs with you, if you have that would be a marvelous beginning," Miss Jackson declared.

"Miss Jackson, anything for you," Edward smiled.

Licking his lips, he leaned over the table and handed Miss Jackson his paystubs. She took them. Edward held her hand longer than he had to. Miss Jackson blushed and her smile came easily.

"Everything looks okay, Mr. Wingate. Just maintain your job and if you have any police contact, please inform me immediately," Miss Jackson said, shuffling through papers, and deliberately not making eye contact with Edward, she added, "Okay sir, that's all. Do you have any questions for me?"

Edward looked deeply into his parole officer's eyes and said seductively, "You said if I had an emergency, I could call you any time day or night. Does that offer still stand?"

Swallowing hard Miss Jackson replied, "Yes Ed, ah, ah… I

mean, Mr. Wingate, it does."

Grabbing her hand to shake it, Edward quickly raised it up to his lips and softly kissed her hand.

"I might just be having an emergency sooner than you think. Take care, Miss Jackson."

"You do likewise," the enchanted parole officer said.

She watched his swagger as Edward Wingate closed the door of Miss Jackson's office. Miss Jackson was finished. She was feeling her new parolee didn't want to stop not even to save her life. Miss Jackson plopped down in her chair and immediately put her hands inside her panties. She was instantly saturated with her own juices. Smiling, she uttered under breath, "Hot-damn! Whew! Mr. Wingate, Mr. Wingate!"

She knew all the visits would happen with no problems. Incarceration shaped Edward into a ruggedly handsome man. Michele Jackson couldn't resist his advances and would sometimes encourage them with a wink or a smile. She didn't do anything to hide the fact that she continuously harbored sexual fantasies about him.

Michele knew it was unprofessional, but couldn't control herself. Ever since Edward Wingate had been assigned to her caseload, the parole officer started mixing business with pleasure. Soon she started to enjoy his bedroom company. It was during these forays that she would often overhear him sleep talking. At first Michele dismissed his behavior, but eventually he was becoming more belligerent in the episodes. One night they had torrid sex and they both went to sleep. She awoke to hear Edward loudly shouting while still asleep.

"Who are you? I can't see your face…"

His eyes were shut and he was fast asleep. Michele felt she had to intercede.

"Ed, Ed, wake up, baby. You were having another nightmare," Michele said, shaking Edward out of another troubling dream.

When she was sure he was alright, Michele went to get him a glass of water. She walked out the bedroom leaving Ed sitting up in bed. He started thinking about all the nightmares he had throughout his life. Now that he knew about his adoption, Ed was convinced his dreams were linked to his biological parents.

Ed went about laying pipe to the total satisfaction of his bedroom partner. Michele Jackson left for work with a glow on her face. Ed took a shower thinking about the decision he had to make regarding finding his biological parents. If he could find them then he could obtain the answers to the question about his adoption. He knew this would end his tormented nights. There wasn't much information to go on, but the name of the adoption agency was known. Once Edward was dressed that was the first place he began in his search.

"I'm sorry Mr. Wingate, but I'm afraid we cannot disclose that information. All our files are strictly confidential."

Edward went to the agency and even though he gave the

names of his adopted parents, all that did was to get the supervisor to call the director. She gave him the negative response. After arguing with the director of the adoption agency for what seemed like hours, Edward walked out in disgust. With the knowledge that his files were in the office he planned on coming back.

For weeks he went back only to receive the same response. Fed up, Ed decided to do what he had to. On the Christmas Eve of the year of his release from prison, he committed his second felony while still on parole. At the agency's annual Christmas party, while staff was in the main dining room celebrating the holidays, Ed slipped undetected in the director's office. It was breaking and entering but he had to see his files.

Larry and Jaqesha Anderson last known address 4270 Avenue D, N.Y. Edward tried to see the name of the borough, unfortunately what looked like coffee stains had spoiled his view of his parents' address, but he knew it was in New York.

Ed had a prostitute from the lower east side who used to talk about how her boys on Avenue D had the bomb dope back in the days. That was his destination.

It was during a blizzard on a Sunday morning. Ed got dressed and boarded the number 2 train at Gun Hill Road station, heading downtown. He always liked to ride the last car on the train.

Because of the weather, the train was damn near empty. In the last car were two drunks along with a middle-aged Hispanic woman, wearing a short skirt with leather jacket. As the train left the station, Ed sat down and closed his eyes. When he opened his eyes, he was in a tunnel and the only passengers left were the woman and himself. She kept glancing Ed's way, all the while adjusting herself in her seat.

The lady got up and walked over to the seat in front of Ed train as the pulled out of 149th and Grand Concourse. She had her back to him and was looking at a train map and also looking at Ed through his reflection in the glass window.

Ed smiled when she bent over putting her face closer to the map as if she was near-sighted. She wasn't wearing any panties and that made Ed laugh. The woman heard his laughter and turned around.

"What's funny, Papi?"

Ed shook his head and said, "Nada, Señorita, I was just wondering how you were going to prevent that sweet pussy of yours from catching a cold?"

The lady smiled at Ed's humor and moved closer to him.

"I don't know, Papi, you have any ideas?"

Ed smiled. "Well, they say sushi should be served chilled. Maybe you got the right idea. Let's talk about it."

Ed glanced in both directions. The adjacent cars were vacant. He smiled while unzipping his pants.

"Ay caramba!" the woman shouted when she saw his long hard penis.

With no other word, the woman started sucking Ed's dick

like a veteran. She had his whole shaft in her mouth and was going for his balls. Ed had been given head from hundreds of women, but this experienced woman was doing work. Ed was about to come when the train pulled into the station. Before it came to a complete stop Ed discharged his entire load into her mouth. The extremely talented head-blower just casually got up off her knees, smiled at Ed and walked off the train with a bellyful of his babies. Ed was fully spent. He smiled, drifting off to sleep.

"Yo homeboy, yo wake up!"

The loud voice startled Edward. Yawning, Ed slowly opened his eyes. Three men were standing over him, looking down at him with mean intentions. One of them sat down next to him.

"What you got, G? I know you got some dough for us," he said.

Edward was nervous. He could see a gun protruding from under one of the men's jackets. Ed worked up enough courage to address the men.

"Pardon me, gentlemen. No disrespect intended, but my monetary units are extremely limited and I really cannot contribute to your cause. I'm sorry."

The men stared at each with perplex exuding from their faces. Then they busted out laughing so hard they had to grab each other from falling over.

"Aw shit, we're robbing Bryant fucking Gumbel!" the man who appeared to be the leader said while laughing.

"Hey, Bryant, do you have any Grey Poupon?" one of his sidekicks added.

The men continued amusing themselves some more. Then suddenly they got serious.

"Well, Bryant, you really gave us a great laugh kid. We needed that in this fucking blizzard, homeboy, plus you got heart, cuz. I like you, homeboy, so this might be your lucky day."

"I'm sorry, sir, but I seem to be at a loss to your meaning," Ed said, staring at the man talking.

"See, that's the shit I'm talking about," the man laughed. "You're just cooler than a fan baby. So check this out, if you can solve this little riddle I throw at you, baby boy, you're free to walk outta here."

The other men started laughing, knowing what riddle their leader was talking about. This was not the first time a potential victim was given this chance. It was their version of Russian roulette. Ed knew if he solved the riddle he would probably be free. If it was wrong he could count on being robbed.

"You ready for this one?" The leader of the stick-up crew asked.

"By all means, sir, proceed," Edward smiled.

The men all smiled at Ed's show of confidence.

"Okay my educated brother, here goes. What's the only living thing on this planet that crawls on all fours in the morning? Walks upright on two legs during midday, then on three legs during the late hours?"

"Yeah, Bryant Gumbel, let's see your smartass get that, playboy," the robber seated next to Ed shouted.

Ed closed his eyes for a few seconds thinking. Then he slowly opened his eyes smiling. "The answer, gentlemen, is Man."

The smiles on the men's faces quickly vanished. "Oh shit he got—"

Cutting off his boy the leader who recited the poem said, "Okay brain, now you finish it up or you lose baby."

"Well gentlemen, you see when a human being is first born, as an infant, it crawls around on all fours, meaning its hands and knees. Then when it reaches a certain age and throughout its middle aged years, it walks erect and upright on two legs. Now as the person gets older, they often need the aid of a cane or crutch to assist in their movement, two legs plus a cane makes three."

It was again Ed's turn to smile. The men looked at each other and smiled, then told Ed, "Yous a bad mother fucker, Bryant. Yo, baby, you free to roll, no charge."

The men then walked toward the next car to look for easier, less educated prey.

"Pardon me, gentlemen, I'm going to Avenue D. What would be the best stop to get off?"

The leader of the pack turned and told Ed. "Yo, get off at 14 street and walk east toward the river. Can't miss it, baby. Peace, Bryant."

Chapter 07

After Edward got off the number 2 train at 14th Street, he walked into a candy store for a pack of gum and to get directions to Avenue D. When he got the directions, Edward started heading east. With each passing block, his anticipation and anxiety grew, and he started to imagine what his biological parents would look like. Edward turned right on Avenue D and started looking for the address he got from his file at the adoption agency. At 12th and Avenue D he still hadn't found the building. In fact the numbers seemed to be way off. He walked two more blocks and no sight of the address. Edward stood on the corner of 10th Street and Avenue D and looked up and down the block. That is when he noticed a middle-age man standing next to a shopping cart staring at him smiling.

Ed frowned up his face before yelling, "Do you find something amusing, sir?"

The man wheeled his cart over to Ed's side of the street and said, "Man, a blind person could see your ass is lost. And brother this ain't the corner to be standing on looking all zoned out, trust me. What you looking for, young fella?"

Edward looked quickly at the paper with the address and said, "4720 Avenue D, sir. Could you tell me if I'm heading in the right direction?"

The man then burst out laughing. "Oh yeah you're heading in the right direction, it's just about four hundred blocks to your left."

The man then turned and pointed off into the distance before adding, "Right across the river."

Ed scowled at the man. Seeing that Ed was not amused the man stopped laughing.

"Young brother, the Avenue D you're looking for is in Brooklyn, not here in Manhattan. I knew people out that way who used to live on the block you're looking for." The man seemed to drift off for a moment recalling a time long ago.

"Brooklyn…? Where in Brooklyn, and how do I get there?"

It started to rain lightly as Edward asked the question. The man gave directions to Ed. He wrote it down on the back of the paper with his parents' name and address. The rain started pelting and the man told Ed he was going to his apartment.

"Listen youngster, it's a long walk to the train in this pouring rain. If you want to, you can come chill at my crib until the rain lets up a bit. It's on you, youngster."

Edward looked suspiciously at the man for a few seconds. He noticed something familiar about him, but could not put his finger on it. The two men were getting soaked standing on the corner. Ed decided to take him up on the offer.

"It ain't much, but it's clean, and for now it's mine," the man said, showing Edward his one-bedroom, basement apartment on 10th Street. He explained to Ed that he was the assistant superintendent for the building. He was able to stay rent-free. In return he had to maintain the entire building.

"Thanks for letting me dry off here, sir. I really appreciate it."

Besides an old mattress in the corner, a small television sitting on a crate, and a lopsided couch, the place was empty. The man walked into the living room after going to the kitchen for two plastic cups of water. Ed noticed the man had a slight limp.

"Have you lived here long, sir?" Ed asked, taking the cup of water.

"Not really, son. I moved to Manhattan some years ago and just haven't been able to get back home yet," the man said, looking at Ed.

Sensing that the man was a little uncomfortable talking about himself, Ed stopped talking, relaxed, and listened to the raindrops.

"Chance, yo, Chance you there?"

Ed was suddenly awakened by someone yelling in the hallway outside the apartment. Realizing that he had dozed off, he immediately jumped up and looked around the room. He was alone. Ed walked into the kitchen and the bathroom. Both were empty. The yelling continued and was now accompanied by knocking. Ed walked to the door and opened it. A tall, balding elderly man was at the door looking at Ed as if he knocked on the wrong door.

"Son, is Chance here? I didn't see his cart outside but I figured I'd check anyway."

Ed examined the balding gentleman for a second before saying, "Well, sir, if you mean the superintendent that lives here, he's not in at the moment. He must have just stepped out."

The man gave Ed a peculiar look. "Super? What super? Chance! Are we talking about the same person, son? A tall man with wavy hair and he has a slight limp…?"

"Yes, sir, that's who I'm referring to… The man who lives here…"

Laughter erupted from the bald man's mouth. He put his hands around Ed's shoulder.

"Son, Chance is no damn superintendent. Shit he can't even

change a light bulb. Chance is just a dope-fiend who crashes here sometimes because the apartment is usually vacant. Didn't you notice there're no locks on the door? Dozens of dope fiends come here daily to fix, this is their hangout."

Ed's golden brown face turned bright red with anger. Shaking his head, Ed grabbed his coat, walking to the door. He was preparing to leave the apartment.

"You better check your pockets young blood. If I know old Chance he got you for his fix money," the old man said and left Ed standing in the doorway.

Ed could hear him laughing as he walked out the back door to the building. Ed put his hand in his jacket pocket, checking for his wallet. Just as the bald man predicted, Ed was a victim of foul play. Chance robbed him.

When Ed reached out into the streets he noticed the rain had melted the snow and the streets were filled with slush. All his money was in his wallet. He couldn't just walk to the train station and continue his journey dead broke. Edward wanted to somehow find Chance and retrieve his chips.

Silently cursing himself for falling asleep in a strange place, Edward walked through unfamiliar streets looking for his pick-pocketing host. He was mad at himself, but this fool had set him up. Being a victim gnawed his mind as he passed an alley on Avenue A. Ed saw the shopping cart parked on the curb. Ed wasn't sure if it belonged to Chance, but he looked down the alley anyway. Hearing voices echoing from the back of the alley, Ed went in and walked toward the rear. The moment he reached the back of the alley he could hear the familiar voice of Chance.

"I hope you have my money, man! That was foul what you did!"

Turning suddenly, Chance and his companion saw Ed staring at them. His eyes were bloodshot with hatred. Instantly knowing what Ed was talking about, the other man told Chance that he had to leave, and quickly left the alley to avoid any conflict. Chance looked at Ed with his glassy, dilated eyes and smiled.

"Well, my young brother, I see that you've found me. I'm sorry, man, but I needed to fix real bad. I had no choice, young blood."

"Listen, fella, just give me back my wallet, and my money, and I'll be on my way. No problems, cool?" Ed said trying hard not to hurt the old man.

Chance smiled and rolled up his tattered jacket sleeve exposing a perforated junkie's arm.

"Well, baby boy, I wish I could. But unfortunately your loot is swimming through these veins as we speak," Chance laughed loudly.

He started to walk away. Ed got furious when the laughter rang out.

"Hey…!" Edward shouted.

He ran up behind Chance further infuriated at being ignored.

Ed spun him around and saw the small knife in Chance's hand. Ed reacted quickly, grabbing Chance's wrist that held the blade and prevented Chance from stabbing him.

The two men struggled, grappling for possession of the weapon. They both fell, slipping on slushy ice. Ed fell on top of Chance then noticed he wasn't moving. When Ed rose to his feet, he did so alone. Chance was lying still on the ground. Ed was in total shock when he looked down on his robber. The knife was protruding from Chance's chest. Ed panicked.

Glancing quickly up and down the alley, Ed saw no one in sight. He reached down and touched Chance's neck to feel for a pulse. Life had left the old pickpocket. Ed thought about his wallet and went through the dead man's pockets. Finding his wallet, it only contained ten dollars. Chance had already shot up over a hundred dollars of Ed's hard earned money. He kept searching and came across an old I.D. He saw Chance's picture and under the photo was the name Chance Williams. Ed looked at the lifeless body for a few moments feeling regret. He then looked around and quickly left the alley hoping his crime went unnoticed.

Chapter 08

The train ride to Brooklyn seemed like an eternity for Edward Wingate. He knew that the body in the alley would not be found for at least a few days, but his paranoia had him feeling like he was a hunted murderer already. Everyone on the walk to the train station and even on the train itself looked like the police to Ed.

He constantly looked at the paper with the directions to his parents' neighborhood that Chance gave him, trying to avoid eye contact with anyone. Ed got off at Newkirk Avenue and asked directions to Avenue D, the Vandeveer Projects.

Ed was closer to his destination and felt the anxiety building inside. The numbers to the houses and buildings were steadily rising as was his anticipation. Ed finally reached 4270. He stood outside the building thinking about the next few minutes when he would be reunited with his biological parents. Entering the lobby, Ed walked over to the intercom directory and looked for the name Anderson.

"Alcott, Almeida, Andrade, damn no Anderson!" Edward mumbled aloud, scrutinizing the names again.

His biological parents' name was absent from the listing. Wondering if he was in the right place, Ed walked back outside and checked his paper for the hundredth time and then looked at the building. He was at the correct address and went back inside. When he entered the building again a heavy set woman was getting off the elevator and looked his way.

"May I help you, young man?"

"Yes, ma'am, actually you can. I was looking for a couple who lives in this building," Ed paused and again looked at his paper. "Larry and Jaqesha Anderson…"

The woman put her head down on hearing the names as she was trying to recollect. Suddenly the woman smiled, remembering and said, "Oh yes, the Andersons a fine couple, but they haven't lived in this building for some time now."

Edward's face got flushed and he asked, "They're no longer here?"

Letting the news sink in, Ed turned toward the directory. "Would you have any idea where they might have moved to, ma'am?"

The woman saw the pain in Ed's eyes. She decided not to let the unpleasant information about the couple slip.

"No, sir, I'm sorry I don't, but I wish you luck. Take care," she said, hurrying out the lobby.

Ed sat on the benches in the projects for hours looking at the building, his thoughts were muddled. If his stomach hadn't loudly growled informing him that it was empty, he would have sat there all night. Ed checked his pockets. After leaving the alley where Chance laid dead, Ed had bought lunch but couldn't eat. Having participated in Chance's death, eating just didn't feel right. He bought two tokens now all he had thirty-six cents.

Ed found himself walking aimlessly down Clarendon Avenue with no destination, money, and worst, no family. He almost collided with a middle-aged woman who came running around the corner. The woman cursed at him.

"Shit, nigger, watch where you going!"

The sound of sirens filled the air. Ed was surprised when the woman, after looking down the block, put her arms around him.

"Keep walking," she said.

They started strolling down the street and the woman began laughing with Ed just like they were old friends. A patrol car came cruising by. Its occupants spotted Ed and the woman. The police cruiser slowed down looked, and kept on driving by.

Looking down the road and making sure the car was out of sight, the woman laughed.

"Damn that was close. I've been ducking 'em crackers all day," she said. Realizing she was still hugging Ed's arm, she let go. "Thanks for having my back, cutie. Good looking out," the woman said walking away. Then she turned back quickly. "Shit, I almost forgot what I'm doing out here. What's up, cutie? You goin' out?"

Ed smiled to himself before addressing the woman's proposition. "Honestly sweetheart, some loving would be very welcomed after a day like I've been having, but this brother is busted so I'll have to decline."

Ed just told her that to be pleasant but he had no intention on purchasing something that he'd gotten his whole life for free. He was a firm believer in the philosophy that a true player would never pay for pussy, but let the pussy pay for him.

"My first priority is nourishment. I'm quite famished."

Looking Ed up and down, trying to figure him out, the woman made another offer.

"Listen cutie, I owe you for having my back, and saving me from a night in central booking. Check it out. I'm kinda hungry myself. I got some leftover chicken and collard greens in my apartment, interested?"

Before Ed could reply his stomach growled. They both laughed and started walking arm in arm.

"Damn brother slow down. You really was starving."

When Ed got to the woman's apartment, she went to take a shower. Jasmine had a very cozy apartment that was well furnished.

Ed felt surprisingly at ease in her company. He sat at the dining table and started eating like a runaway slave. When his hostess came out the shower he was still at it.

"I'm glad that you're enjoying my food, cutie." Then she added, "Hey, I don't even know your name."

Ed looked up from his plate with chicken grease all over his face. "Please excuse my manners, Edward Wingate at your service, Miss."

She blushed at Ed's politeness and killer smile. Extending her hand the woman returned the formalities.

"Mister, you can call me Jasmine. And it's a pleasure to make your acquaintance."

The two new friends spent the rest of the evening talking, laughing and listening to music.

After sharing a bottle of wine, Jasmine went into her bedroom. Later she emerged wearing only panties and a bra. Her openness did not affect Ed and he thoroughly examined her body.

"Damn, girl, for a dinosaur your body is well preserved."

"Dinosaur...? You got some nerves!"

Jasmine ran after Ed, chasing him and laughing. They both ran straight into the bedroom. Ed proceeded to run straight up inside of Jasmine. Ed gave Jasmine loving that she hadn't had in years, and instantly she was whipped. Jasmine soon asked Ed to move in with her and to be her man. Ed had nothing in the Bronx except a parole violation. He hoped to get information about his parents in Brooklyn and accepted.

"Just come on the track with me tonight and watch my back, please baby," Jasmine said.

She was getting dressed one night to go up on the whore stroll. She wanted to show Ed to her co-workers.

"Okay, let's see if you know how to get that paper, or you just play-fucking for lunch money."

Jasmine looked at Ed and smiled then said, "Damn, brother, talking that slick shit, I'd swear your fine ass was some kinda pimp and shit."

Ed smiled back at his lady and held out his hand before saying, "May I re-introduce myself. I'm Ed Lover pimp and player extraordinaire at your service. Now let's go get my paper, bitch!"

Jasmine burst out in laughter. She hugged Ed tightly and said, "Yeah, Daddy, let's go get your paper! You sweet talking, sweet dick macaroni you…"

It was on and poppin'. The whore stroll accepted Ed with open arms and legs. Many of the ladies of the evening were freelance warriors, but they were in search of a competent and skilled pimp. After seeing how Ed managed Jasmine's career, a few of her co-workers put in their application. For the third time in his life, Edward Wingate found himself in the flesh peddling business. Jasmine proved to be a very competent bottom whore. Supervising Ed's staff proficiently and kept order around the stable. Unfortunately, for Jasmine and Ed, they broke a cardinal rule of Pimpology—they started to fall hard for each other. After Ed started pimping hard in Brooklyn and being in the streets on a regular, he knew he had to change his look, especially after his ordeal on the lower east side.

"Baby, what did you do to your hair?" Jasmine said, referring to Ed's new look. As he entered the house she noticed he cut off his long dreadlocks.

"Just changing it up a bit, boo. You like?"

Jasmine walked over to the front door and hugged her man before saying, "Locks or no locks, you look damn fine." Then she whispered seductively, "Hey, handsome, you mind helping me cut my hairs?" Looking deeply into Ed's eyes Jasmine moaned, "Especially my pubic hairs."

Immediately Jasmine took Ed's hand and put it down inside her panties. She wore a smile as Ed led her into the bedroom. Lying in bed, both were spent from the passionate love they made. Ed kicked back while Jasmine cuddled up next to him. Jasmine kissed Ed's neck and then started licking his ear. Ed was enjoying the afterplay then Jasmine suddenly stopped. He saw a strange look on her face.

"What's up, boo? Did I forget to wash behind my ear or something?"

Jasmine was in a deep and distant thought. She did not laugh at his attempted humor. Ed stood up and asked, "What's going on, Jas? You okay?"

"Yeah, I'm fine, baby. I was just thinking about something,"

Jasmine smiled, coming out of her private thoughts.

She stopped talking and Ed saw the tears forming in her eyes. Jasmine turned to Ed. held his hand and said, "Ed, I never told you this, but I was married once. I was happily married to a wonderful man. Everything was going great until I got pregnant."

Staring at Ed, Jasmine watched Ed's reaction. His soft, understanding smile told her to go on.

"Baby, because of circumstances we gave up our baby for adoption. A weird feeling came over me while I was licking your ear. I saw your birthmark behind your left ear. And well, seeing that just brought back all these memories."

Ed looked at her confused.

"Baby, why would my birthmark trigger those memories?"

"You see Ed... My baby had a similar mark. It was like a butterfly behind his left ear."

Ed looked shock and stunned by the news. He instinctively put his hand on the left side of his head, while staring dumbfounded at Jasmine.

"Really...?"

"Yes and even though it was so long ago, I still remember it like it was yesterday."

Jasmine started crying slightly and Ed embraced her. He was hoping she wouldn't stop, but wanted her to tell him more. She did.

"That's not all, boo. After we gave him up for adoption, we

had terrible regrets and that's when our life and marriage changed," Jasmine sighed.

She had Ed's full attention and they both slowly stood and got out of the bed. Ed picked up a glass of water and sipped. Jasmine started putting on her clothes, but continued with her story.

"Baby, I think it was the stress or the guilt that caused my husband to start using drugs. He became a dope addict and eventually ran off to be with one of his mistress. He's with that bitch heroin. He moved to Manhattan and changed his name to Chance. And I never saw his ass again."

Ed dropped the glass of water he was drinking and stared at Jasmine in shock. The disturbed look on Ed's face made Jasmine move closer to him.

"Baby, what's wrong?" She asked with concern.

Ed was trembling. He tried to open his mouth nothing came out. What was going on in his mind was heavy and held his tongue under duress. Ed was praying it was all just a big coincidence. He heard Jasmine's voice.

"Ed, baby, talk to me, what is it?"

Ed, who never touched alcohol, walked to the liquor cabinet and poured himself a glass of scotch. He sipped the warm liquor to settle his nerves. Staring at Jasmine with wide-eyed amazement, he painfully told her what was troubling him.

"Remember when we first met and I told you I was on the run for some bullshit? Well, it really was a lot more serious than that,"

Ed said.

Jasmine held Ed's trembling hands. Feeling how scared he was, she tried to console him.

"Ed, just tell me what it is, baby. It will make you feel better to talk about it. Please my baby, talk to me."

He took another drink of the numbing brew before saying, "Baby, I killed a man."

There was a shocked expression on Jasmine's face. Ed held her hand tighter and continued with the story.

"The man I killed ah, his name was Chance."

Jasmine was numb and didn't say anything at first. She could see by Ed's expression he thought the murdered man and her husband were the same person. She thought more and more, her denial helped her to arrive at other possibilities. Holding Ed close, Jasmine smiled and said, "Baby, do you know how many Chances there are living in this city? Hell, even in Manhattan alone, there must be a few dozen. It's so unlikely the man you're talking about is actually my husband. Besides I always used to dream that one day my husband would come limping back into my life. My dreams usually come true."

Ed's mouth dropped open and gently pushed Jasmine away. He stared into her soft brown eyes.

"What did you say? What did you mean limp back into your life?"

Feeling uneasy Jasmine put a smile on her face. She was

trying to hide the concern in her heart. Jasmine was doing it more for her sake than Ed's.

"It was just a joke, baby. Chance had a slight limp that I used to tease him about. That's all."

"Oh my, fucking God! Oh no, it can't be," Ed shouted and started shivering uncontrollably.

He sat down on a sofa. Jasmine ran over and knelt in front of Ed.

"Baby, what's wrong?" she asked.

Ed put his hands over his head and yelled, "The Chance I killed had a limp, that's what the fuck is wrong."

"Oh…"

Jasmine almost fainted in Ed's lap. When Ed looked at her, she was milk white and a look of terror clouded her face. Ed kneeled down next to Jasmine and put his arms around her body.

"Oh, Jasmine, I'm so sorry, baby. I'd do anything to change what I did. I love you, Jas. Please talk to me, baby."

Endless thoughts ran through Jasmine's mind. Her mind set her back on the boardwalk at Coney Island. It was that accursed night. In her head, she heard the old mystic telling her all about her unborn son. She remembered holding her baby boy, discovering, and kissing his birthmark. Jasmine's distraught mind envisioned that she was hugging her baby in one hand and embracing Ed her lover in the other.

"Jasmine, what are you thinking about baby? Do you hear

me? Talk to me, please."

Slowly Jasmine's eyes focused on Ed and she cried out.

"Ed, don't say a word, just listen. I'm afraid what you did to my husband might be more than just a coincidence," Jasmine said, holding Ed close. She told him the story of the mystic fortuneteller from Coney Island.

"That's crazy. You really believed that old man? Listen, baby, just get control of yourself and hear me out. I agree there are some coincidences, like the adoption and the birthmark. And yes, even the limp. I will give all that, but check this out and this will put everything in the right perspective and then you can stop being so superstitious. Jasmine listen, I went to the adoption agency when I got out of prison and I got the names and address of my real parents. Rest assured that Chance and you are not my parents. So stop it, baby. Please," Ed said.

There seemed to be a look of relief on Jasmine's face. Ed got up and walked to the kitchen. He turned back suddenly and said, "Now, when we get all this drama behind us what you could do is help me locate my real parents. Their names are Larry and Jaqesha Anderson."

"Ah-ah-ah…" Jasmine screamed, jumping up off the floor.

The blood curdling sound made it appeared that her soul was leaving her body. She screamed again, and the terror-filled shrieks chilled Ed's bone to the marrow. Jasmine pushed Ed away as he tried to grab her. She ran to get her coat and purse.

"Jasmine, where are you going?" Ed shouted after her.

At this point, Jasmine's mind was totally distorted. She ran to the door, opened it, and rushed out into the hallway all the while screaming, "Oh my God, it's true…! The curse, it's true!"

Ed tried chasing her but he slipped on a wallet that fell from her purse. She fled the apartment. Ed twisted his ankle on the fall. He gingerly stood with the wallet in his hand. Ed limped over to the sofa and sat in agonizing pain. He took off his shoes and socks to see if his ankle was swollen.

Ed opened Jasmine's wallet. Looking through the contents he saw several sleeves that were filled with credit cards and a library card. Ed searched the back of the wallet where he found a picture of Jasmine and her husband. It was the man he had killed. Ed continued his search and saw a small picture behind the first one. He took it out and examined it closely. It was a picture of a younger looking Jasmine, but unmistakably her. It was an old driver's license picture.

Ed looked at the name and address under the photo, Jaqesha Anderson, 4720 Avenue D, Brooklyn, N.Y. Ed's mind cracked at that moment and he sat there in a catatonic state. All of the events that happened in his life melted his mind. Most of his life he spent having nightmares or wondering about his parents' and his real identity. His journey was long and sometimes rough, but now his quest was over. Edward Wingate, or Edward Anderson, could now end the search. He found out who he was. What he was, a curse.

EPILOGUE

"All we have to do now is fill out your W2 form. Then I'll take you on a tour of the facilities. We're very happy to have you on our team," Mr. Bennett said.

The director of Happy Acres Psychiatric Hospital was just finishing up the final paperwork with a nurse the facility recently hired. Mr. Bennett took the new staff member on a tour of the grounds and introduced her to the staff and several patients. He then went over her patients' evaluations and treatment plans.

"Okay, this gentleman is your last patient. He was found walking aimlessly through the streets of Brooklyn. He was incoherent and apparently recently had a severe psychiatric breakdown, and hasn't spoken a word since the authorities brought him here. Since then he has been admitted for further test and evaluation."

Before the director and his new employee entered the patient's room, he stopped her at the door.

"Here he is. I'll leave you alone to evaluate his condition for yourself. Then I will meet you back at my office, okay?"

"That will be fine, sir. I'll be there shortly."

The director walked away, thinking about how it would feel to make love to his sexy new employee. Entering the patient's room, the nurse stood there for a few seconds looking at him. He was helplessly sitting there and tears started to well up in her eyes.

In a chair looking out the window with a blank disconnected stare on his face, Edward Anderson-Wingate moved his head slightly after hearing footsteps. The night that his mysterious origin unfolded, Edward found out the real truth about his parents. The shock of being his mother's lover and father's murderer hit him hard and caused his hospitalization. He had walked the streets of Brooklyn in a semi-catatonic state for a few days before being confronted by the police for loitering.

Edward's nurse walked over to the window and looked at her patient then smiled.

"Hey, Lover, how have you been? Baby, I've been so worried about you. After you got arrested and was sent upstate, no one heard anything about you for years," the nurse said, sitting down in a chair next to Ed.

She reached and took his hand in hers. He looked in her direction but the blank, indifferent stare did not change.

"Ed after I stopped selling my body, I went to nursing school, and graduated with honors. All through those years I never stopped inquiring and looking for you, but I kept coming up empty."

The nurse stopped talking and leaned over looking into Ed's eyes. There was a helpless look on his face and it caused her tears to come down steadily.

"Ed... Daddy, it's crazy, but when a nurse friend of mine told me about a new patient and described him to me, I knew it was you. So here I am. Damn I missed you, Ed," the nurse said, getting up and walking over to the bed to regain her composure.

Lying on the bed was an old *Daily News*. The headline caught her attention. She picked up the newspaper and read.

Woman was found hanging from a tree in Prospect Park. Death ruled to be suicide. Authorities who found the body recognized her as a known prostitute from the Vandeveer projects area in Brooklyn. Although there was no identification found on the body local officers knew her as Jasmine.

Finding out the predictions she received at Coney Island so long ago were being lived out was too much for Jaqesha Anderson, AKA Jasmine, to bear. She took her own life instead of living with the shame of being, both sexual lover and natural mother to the same man. The nurse went back over to the window. Holding his hands again she put one to her lips and kissed it.

"Daddy, I'm here and here I'm staying. I got a job as your nurse and I'm going to nurse your fine ass back to health, I promise."

Getting excited the nurse added, "Daddy, this facility is a gold mine. I can get paid with these lame ass doctors. You should have seen them drooling over this body when I first walked into the hospital. When they sample this bomb ass pussy and my killer head game a sister's gonna have to hire an accountant to monitor my cash flow." Looking at her watch and standing up, the nurse started to laugh. "Daddy, I have to go to work. I'm gonna stop by that cornball director's office and lighten his load and his pockets for him." Leaning over to kiss Ed, the nurse squeezed his hand. "I'll be back later, to check on you, daddy."

Walking to the door the nurse stopped short, thinking she heard a sound coming from Ed. Dismissing it, she started to open the door. The low whisper became a little louder but still unrecognizable. The nurse turned around and walked back to Ed's chair. The low-pitched sounds were coming out of Ed's partially closed mouth. The nurse's eyes widened at the realization of his potential breakthrough. Ed was communicating.

"Yes daddy, it's me. Talk to me, Ed Lover. You can do it. Please daddy, keep trying."

The nurse placed her ear closer to Ed's lips. At first, the sounds were garbled and meaningless, but as the nurse listened longer, the sounds started to form into recognizable words. The words slowly turned into a phrase that brought a smile to her pretty face.

Edward Anderson Wingate squeezed his nurse's hand and

whispered, "Yeah bitch, go get my money."

Miss Branch threw her hands around her old pimp, Ed Lover. She fervently kissed him repeatedly. She eventually stood up and walked to the door. Before leaving she turned and said, "Okay Daddy, I'll be back with your trap money. I love you, Ed."

Nurse Branch, also known as Princess, went into the hospital to make her rounds. Her rounds however were not the normal rounds that a nurse would make during the course of her shift. Nurse Branch made office rounds, back stairwell rounds, vacant operating room rounds, broom closet rounds, rooftop rounds, and even parking lot rounds.

Wherever there was a doctor, nurse, male or female, orderly, kitchen worker, janitor or even patients that needed her special services, Nurse Branch was there to do what she did best, fuck for that paper!

THE END

Introduction

In our existence as mortals, we are constantly faced with various tests, and choices that will not only affect our lives, but also the people around us. Most of these tests and choices are usually not life threatening or irreversible. What if there came a time in your life when you are suddenly faced with a choice that could have monumental and even everlasting consequences? Would you choose carefully or be reckless with your life? If you are ever faced with such a choice during your brief lifespan on this temporary plain of existence, please open up your minds and hearts and choose

DEAD AND STINKIN' DE
AD AND STINKIN' DE
NKIN' DE

UNTIL DEATH
DO US PART

Chapter 01

The summer's heat was causing the rancid odor from piled up garbage to emanate throughout the city. This was not the fragrance that two people in the midst of lovemaking wanted to smell. Mike was in the process of heartily sexing his vivacious girl, Laura. Suddenly the pungent odor hit them. Mike was the type of man who liked to joke around with his woman and couldn't let this opportunity pass.

"Damn, you smelling kinda ripe down there. Let me go get the hose," Mike said, getting out of bed.

He felt a blow to the back of the head and turned to see the remote control for the television on the floor next to him.

"Oh, you got jokes, huh? You know that smell is the damn garbage outside! This sanitation strike is really getting out of hand. But since you think it's my coochie that smells like that, let's see when's the next time you'll get to hit it," Laura said, going into the bathroom.

"Stop playing girl. You know I'm just buggin' out with my baby. Your stuff could smell like a dead bullfrog, I'm a still stick my tongue up in your fine ass," Mike said, flickering his tongue like a snake.

Mike and Laura had been friends and lovers for many years. They were deeply in love most of that time. Laura came out the bathroom smiling. Mike's comments had her cracking up. She then went back into the bed and cuddled next to her man.

"A bullfrog huh…? Damn you so nasty," teased Laura.

"No, not nasty… Just in love," Mike smiled.

Laura planted a kiss on Mike's forehead and quickly changed the subject.

"Baby the houses in Soundview are almost on empty and Stephan called from Throgs Neck complaining that the last batch of smoke was kind of weak. We better step our game up," Laura said to her lover and business partner, while rubbing his back.

"Okay boo, I'll bark on those coconuts about the last batch we purchased. And I'll drop off a few dozen pounds in the 'View later this evening. Today however, I would like the honor of taking my best girl out to eat."

"That's sweet baby, after you beat up my little kitty cat all morning, it's only right that you feed a sister. What was up with you anyway? You acted like you were driving a damn truck inside of me, shifting gears and shit," Laura laughed, fanning her vagina area with her hand.

"You don't call me Big Daddy Love Organ for nothing," Mike smiled, gently kissing his woman.

"No matter how many times we come to the Seaport it feels like it's our first date," Laura said.

"I know, baby. It's so laid back and low key, it's just what we need to escape the drama of the projects."

Mike and Laura often escape from their hustling in the Bronx by going on short excursions to Manhattan. They would spend time alone and enjoy each other without the annoying hassle of street life. After a relaxing evening at the South Street Seaport the couple drove back to the Bronx to check on mutual business ventures. Pulling up to a corner on Randall Avenue, they called out to one of their crew leaders.

"Yo Old School, what's up? I see you got the kids with you today."

Before Old School walked to Mike's vehicle he instructed two of his eight kids to wait for him on the benches.

"There's gold in them there hills," Old School shouted, handing Laura a bag full of money he took from his coat pocket. "Yo the block is jumping today but both apartments are almost on empty. A few people complained about the smoke, but it's still moving well. I hope you get some better material this go round, or else," Old School said with a fake screw-face.

"Or else what, cutie…? Are you gonna leave the team and go do your own thing?" Laura asked, pinching Old School's arm.

"Imagine that. I'd first stick my hand in a fan than leave my family. But just step up the quality of the product," Old School replied.

"Go ahead, open up the trunk and grab the duffle bag. I think your people will be happy," Mike said to his main man before driving off.

"Hey, hey, hey, Get Money Crew," Mike shouted, walking into a stash house.

The one bedroom place was located inside a project apartment building. Mike walked in to see the remaining bosses in his crew taking care of business. He had dubbed them The Get Money crew. They were mid-level marijuana organization Mike and Laura started years ago.

Black Rob, Stack Money, Pretty Boy, and Old School were all main players in the organization. They ran dozens of weed houses in various projects in the Bronx. They all had their own crew of workers that reported to them directly. It was the habit however, for the entire management staff to get together once a week and tally up the week's receipts. They also re-stocked their weed supply for their troops.

"What's up boss and boss lady, enjoy y'all day off?" Pretty Boy greeted the couple, entering the stash spot.

"No doubt, Pretty Boy. We always do. So how we looking my brothers can we retire yet?" Mike asked, picking up a stack of hundred dollar bills.

"Not yet, boss... But we definitely on that paper chase," Stack Money exclaimed, counting a pile of dough.

"Rob, why you so quiet, is everything ok?" Laura asked, sensing that the vibes coming from Black Rob wasn't feeling right.

"Yeah, it's all good, you know? Just got some shit on my mind. That's all. We did okay this week, but we could be doing a lot better," Rob mumbled with a troubled look on his face.

Mike felt the tension and broke the ice when he said, "Well my brothers, I've decided to give the entire posse a raise. Even the workers in each of your crews..."

"Hey..." a chorus went up.

"Good looking out, boss. That's what I'm talking about," Pretty Boy said with a big grin.

"Yeah, thanks boss. The extra loot will be right on time," Stack Money said, looking at Black Rob.

"Yo, don't forget we all have to be out at the big park in Castle Hill early Sunday morning. We have to set up for that carnival.

Everyone knows their jobs and responsibilities so let's make this year real special for the shorties and their families," Mike said.

Mike, Laura and the Get Money Crew not only ran a lucrative weed business, they were also responsible for funding many organizations. Mike and Laura loved their communities and the residents love them right back. They used their resources rebuilding and renovating parks, community centers and homeless shelters. Their group also sponsored afterschool and weekend youth programs. They also ran a summer sleep away camp. The crew was doing great business and wonderful things for the community, and everything was running smooth like a well oiled machine. But things were about to change.

Chapter 02

"Damn Mike, I can smell that gage in the trunk all through the jeep," a nervous Laura said from the passenger seat.

"There's no pleasing some people. You complain about the last shipment of smoke, so then I screamed on Dread about it. Now when I get this high grade weed you beef about the smell. Just sit back and be easy, Laura. We're almost there," Mike said.

Laura cautiously glanced out the window for any signs of the police. Mike had made a stop and spoke to his Jamaican connect. They arranged for him to receive a potent shipment of some yard weed to make up for the last batch. Mike phoned ahead to have Black Rob and Pretty Boy meet him downstairs. They could help bring the product up to the stash spot. When the product got upstairs to the apartment, everyone commented on the strong smell.

"The quicker we break down these bales into pounds, the faster we can get them on the street and air out the apartment properly," advised Laura, setting out the triple beam scales for weighing the weed.

"Old School, this should put everything right back on track with the customers. I hope they appreciate the trouble I went through to get this high grade," Mike said to Old School while the rest of the crew was bagging up the weed.

"Damn I almost forgot, fam. Some cats setup shop in Monroe under the breezeway. They got a decent size crew, and I hear their smoke is sump'n exotic."

Hearing what Old School told Mike, Black Rob broke out and said, "Oh hell no! Them niggas got it messed up. Monroe is my set, and I'll be damned if it's going down like that."

Rob pulled his gun from his waist and stared down the barrel. He released the clip and examined it.

"Yo Black, after we finish here let's roll through Monroe and spit some pebbles at them clowns. Let them know shit's real in the field," added Stack Money.

"Hold up Wyatt Earp. There's no need for gunplay at this point. I've been in the game for a while and done seen crews come and go. Unless they're trying to flood the whole projects, a little competition is good for business. It will add a variety of weed to the area and generate more customers and cash flow," Mike said to his crew. "Cool heads will prevail," he smiled.

"Preach that economics shit, you Community College graduate you," applauded Laura, proud of her man's logical reasoning.

"Fuck that! No disrespect to you two, but that's my projects. It's my paper that'll be short, not yours. I'm gonna defend mines. Please believe that," Rob said, heading toward the door. Stack Money was trailing him.

"Easy, Butch and Sundance… Don't go shooting up Dodge City just yet. Let's give it a few weeks and see how this whole thing affects our cash flow. Then we can rethink our position," said Mike.

"Yeah whatever, Mike! You can say what you want. I know what I got to do," Black Rob said to Mike. He turned to Stacks Money and said, "Come on Stacks we out." Black Rob started to walk away, but before leaving he turned around said, "Mike, now that you're paid, it seems like you forgot how to bust your gun. Where did your heart go, player?"

Rob exited the apartment smiling. Everyone there knew that what Rob said was very disrespectful. But Mike let him walk out without any beef. It was true that in his earlier years as a hustler Mike was quick to pick up his burner. Laura was now in his life and with his large stash made him complacent. He was more reluctant to invite violence into his life. The crew looked at each other and bagged up the remaining weed in silence.

"Yo Stacks, turn off the headlights and pull down that side street," Rob ordered, inserting another clip into his assault weapon. "Y'all think shit don't stink? Just check this out, niggas!" shouted Black Rob.

They were in the back of Monroe projects. Black Rob and Stacks Money rolled up on a rival drug crew. The unsuspecting hustlers didn't have a chance as shots rang out under the breezeway. Black Rob's Tech 9 did the rest of the talking, spitting mad rounds. Stack Money let his shotgun erupted in a violent roar. A few of the rivals got hit and many ran away.

"Yeah cowards, remember Black Rob runs this shit. Stay gone or stay dead!" shouted Black Rob.

"I thought I told you two no gunplay!"

Mike, Black Rob and Stacks Money were inside the stash house. Mike was so livid he couldn't sit. He was hopping mad and Laura vainly tried to cool him down. The streets had gotten hot after the shooting in Monroe. The rumor mill had it that Mike's crew was behind the shooting. This caused unwanted friction between

Mike and the community leaders. The result was that his weed operation had to be temporarily shut down. He called two of his street lieutenants in for a meeting. He did not make any effort to hide his displeasure.

"Now look what you did. We gotta lay-low and nobody can get paid because of you two knuckleheads," screamed a furious Mike.

"Hold up Mike, I ain't gonna be too many more knuckleheads, and what is done is done. This shit will blow over soon and it's back to business. Only this time we have one less drug crew to worry about," replied Black Rob.

"Rival crew or not, we're fuckin' sizzlin'. Po-po wants the shooters. And we have no fuckin' dough coming in," fumed Laura.

"I may have an answer to our cash flow problem. You want to tell 'em 'bout it Stacks?"

"It's like this y'all," Stack Money started nervously speaking. He paused before continuing. "Me and Rob ran into this Dominican cat we knew from Rikers Island. And he done blew up big time. Anyway, he told us he would front us some bricks of that powder for a real sweet price."

"And coke money is way longer than this short weed paper. I figure we could make up our losses in just a few days. It's time we started getting major chips like the rest of these crews out here," added Rob, interrupting Stack Money.

"Yo, you two are buggin'. Do you remember we had this talk

at the beginning of our business agreement? When you, Stacks and Pretty Boy joined the crew it was a marijuana crew. That's how this organization started and that's how it's gonna stay. But I'm not on any Nazi dictator shit, so let's all talk about it. Pretty Boy what do you think?"

"For real Mike, I love selling weed. This is a low-key operation. I ain't greedy for no long paper. Coke and dope's what's poppin'. If we don't sell it, someone else will. I can go either way on that, player."

"Fair enough… Old School, holla at your boy," said Mike to his longtime O.G. friend.

"Mike we family, baby. So your call is my call. I got eight kids. I'd really hate to be the cause of them messin' with that p-funk, or them jellybeans. So you can keep it strictly smoke for me," Old School said, smiling and looking at Black Rob.

"I already know where you stand Stacks. If Rob says do it you're down no questions asked. I don't need your feedback. Laura, what you think?"

"You're my man and I'll stand by you all day. It's whatever you decide… I'm ridin' till I die," said Laura, Mike's lifelong girlfriend and right-arm assistant.

"I guess we'll be remaining a marijuana crew. The final decision is mine. I say we stay as is, okay Black Rob?"

"For now player, okay. But before I leave, tell me why you and Laura are so dead set against selling drugs. I never heard of a crew that started off selling smoke and just stayed with smoke. That's ass backwards if you ask me. I gotta move on with the times, kid. Peace I'm out."

Black Rob, Stack Money, and Pretty Boy walked out of the stash house. There was a deep divide remaining behind.

"Baby I ain't trustin' that Rob right about now. I think we need to keep a very close eye on his shiesty-ass," a worried Laura said to her man.

"Don't sweat Black Rob. He's just uptight because his money is funny and his change is strange," laughed Old School, interrupting Laura.

Laughter exploded amongst the three close friends and business associates. . They quickly got serious when Old School spoke again.

"Rob has a point, you two stay away from coke and heroin like they acid or some shit like that. Our crew's about helpin' the community. I know, a little bit of weed never hurt anyone. I'm with the weed hustlin' all day. Just that I think it a little strange that you never once dabbled in hard drugs."

Mike glanced at Laura, then back at Old School before saying, "That's a personal issue for me and Laura. Please just stick with us and our decisions. You've always been my main man."

"No doubt, boss. Well, I gotta bounce up out here, you two. I have to take one of my sons to his basketball game. Be easy. Don't sweat nada," reassured Old School, shaking hands with Mike and embracing Laura.

Alone in the stash house, Mike and Laura sensed things in the organization were about to change. How and when they didn't know. Nobody in the crew knew why the couple never sold hardcore drugs. The deep rooted reason was that Laura's mother and Mike's father were both drug addicts. Laura's mom died of AIDS. She was infected with a contaminated needle she shared with a dope fiend who was HIV positive.

Mike's father was a cocaine addict whose heart gave out while on a smoking binge. The two met at a seminar about deadly drugs. The pair fell in love after a couple meetings. They vowed never to use or sell the drugs that killed their parents. This was a way of honoring their dead parents.

Coming out of their separate thoughts, Laura looked into Mike's eyes and started to cry. Mike held his woman close. Without her speaking he felt what was in her heart. He looked into his woman's eyes and said, "I know baby, it won't be much longer, I'm getting tired of all this mess too."

Chapter 03

The Miami sun burned fiercely on the sand. Mike and Laura were in the midst of enjoying a vacation in South Beach. After the drama with the shootings and the disagreement with Black Rob, Mike decided to take off with Laura. They wanted to unwind and leave all the madness behind.

"Honey you sure know what I need and when I need it. This vacation was right on time, thanks baby," said Laura, opening two bottles of Heineken.

"You know I love you, right baby?" said Mike, looking deep into Laura's eyes and taking his beer.

"Yeah I know, sweetheart," replied Laura.

"When we get back to the city, we're going to tie up some loose ends and hustle for six months. Then we're out of the game for good, okay?"

"Mike, are you serious? I've waited so long to hear you say that. Hell yeah, that's okay with me. And with all the drama, it's right on time," sang Laura.

They spend one more night in South Beach and the couple headed back to New York. Mike and Laura were met by serious changes within the Get Money Crew.

"Pull over here cabbie," Mike told the cab driver.

He had hired the driver at the airport to take him and Laura to the Bronx. The cab pulled over at the corner of Castle Hill and Randall Avenues. They saw things that just didn't look right. Pretty Boy and two of his workers were standing on the corner, Gucci down from head to toe. A customer approached Pretty Boy and handed him a fifty-dollar bill. Instead of handing her the regular, Pretty Boy gave her a clear bag filled with a white milky substance. Mike stared at Laura then rolled down the window.

"Yo Pretty Boy, lemme holla at you real quick," said Mike.

"What's up y'all?" said Pretty Boy, sticking his head in the cab window.

"What's up with you, Pretty Boy? I know I just didn't see what I thought I saw…?"

"Ah hem… Ah…the bosses are back and looking tan and healthy…" said Pretty Boy, struggling for an answer.

"What da—"

"What the fuck did you give that woman?" hollered Mike, cutting off Laura before she could ask the same question.

"Mike, be easy, player. Black Rob said he was trying out something new in your absence. And player it's off the chain. In the two weeks that you've been away, we've been getting paid in full. I bought a ride, new gear, and even hit my crew off with extra loot. Mike, Black Rob was right. We should've been selling coke and dope all along."

Mike was too furious to respond. He stared blankly at Laura and she said what he was thinking.

"Pretty Boy, meet us at the house in an hour. We need to discuss a few things," Laura instructed Pretty Boy with a pleasant attitude. "Contact Black Rob and Stack Money, we're gonna swing by Old School and pick him up, okay?"

"Sure, sure boss lady, it's done. See you in an hour."

Walking away from the cab, Pretty Boy strolled over to his new Nissan Maxima and jumped in. He drove off.

"Damn honey! What've these niggas done?" inquired Laura, grabbing her head as if it hurt. She looked at Mike. "Let's just go snatch up Old School and see what the deal is."

"I told 'em fuckas, they were fuckin' crazy to flip the script like that while you were on vacation. Rob and Stacks just laughed and kept on doing their thing. Mike, they flooded four different projects with dope and coke. There's been a couple of shootouts with rival crews. And what's worse, they're still claiming they down with Get Money. So now this looks like it's your doing," explained Old School.

He ran down everything that had been going on during Mike and Laura's absence. Mike was about to make a comment when the door to the apartment opened. In walked Black Rob, Stack Money and Pretty Boy. All three decked out in expensive gear and crazy iced-out jewelry. Rob walked into the living room, showing off his grill of gold teeth.

"Hey boss and boss lady, what's shaking? I hope you enjoyed your vacation. I know you can see we've made some minor changes."

"Yeah Rob, I saw some of your changes up in Castle Hill. Old School's been filling me in on the rest," replied Mike, trying to keep his composure.

"School didn't agree with our changes, and he decided to stick to his tired old weed hustle. That's cool, but the rest of us had to step our game up a bit," said Black Rob, screwing up his face at Old School.

"Yeah, well School is loyal to the end. So what he did doesn't surprise me. But you cats done lost your damn minds. I told you to lay-low until we get back. Then five-Oh would've eased up the pressure. What do you do? You open up a fucking drug store. Alright, listen here Black Rob since you started this madness, I want you to fuckin' clean up the shit. Take all that shit off my streets and resume normal operations. Or you can find yourself another crew to run with," warned Mike.

"Oh you got jokes? Sorry big dog, but the wheels already in motion. There's too much paper at stake to back out now. Things will remain the way they are. But I'll tell you what I'll do better than just leave this sorry ass crew. I'll start my own drug cartel… These fuckin' streets will be mine!"

"Your greed is gonna be your downfall, Rob. Believe that," warned Laura.

Ignoring her Rob continued, "It's been real, Mike. But me and the crew have to roll. We got real shit to handle."

Black Rob, Stack Money and Pretty Boy exited the apartment with wide grins on their faces.

"If he thinks he's gonna keep pushing that death in our hood, he's crazy," said Mike. Laura and Old School looked at him shaking their heads. "School, we gonna drop Laura off then roll on the blocks and set shit straight. We'll try and do it without any gunplay."

"Mike, these cats ain't gangsters, but when all this money is at stake, cats ain't playin' around either. They've tasted real cash and they're not just gonna give that up without a fight. Now Mike, I know how you feel about drama. So let me go to Bed-sty and round up my old hit squad to roll with us in case there's any resistance," pleaded Old School.

"Not just yet, Dillinger. Let's try it my way first. We'll go into the projects and take as much of that garbage out of the hood as possible. Then we'll wait and see whether Rob wants to go to war, or have a sit down, and negotiate the alternatives."

"Okay boss, it's your call. But I'm strapping up heavy anyway," said Old School, checking his 9mm. He went to the wall safe and retrieved the Desert Eagle.

"Baby, I have a bad feeling. Please be careful and come home early tonight," begged Laura with tears in her eyes.

"Don't worry, I got this lover. I'll be home before you go to sleep. I promise you. Let's roll School."

Laura was dropped off at the house as planned. Then Mike and Old School ran through four housing projects and literally robbed all the rouge Get Money workers selling rock and powder. Before the sun came up the next morning Mike and Old School had damn near cleared out all the coke, and dope in the projects.

"School, be easy gangster. You a bad boy with 'em guns. I forgot how ill you used to be when you was a stickup kid," said Mike, leaving Old School at his house.

"Boss, it's done, but I can tell you it's not over. Them dudes ain't gonna sit still and take what we did lightly. Be on your guard and I'll holla at you later," said Old School.

He went into the house but came back out after he was sure

that Mike had driven away.

"Where the hell have you been? Do you know how much tears the human body can produce?" Not waiting for Mike to respond Laura continued. "Well I do, because I've been worried to death and crying for hours. Baby why didn't you call? I've been going crazy thinking the worst," said a trembling Laura, hugging Mike.

"I'm sorry. Just got caught up with School, and taking back the streets mission I been on. I'm sorry that I had you so worried."

"How did it go, Mike?" asked Laura, trying to be calm.

"We did what we planned on doing. Now we'll wait and see what Rob's reply will be."

"I have a good idea what it's gonna be Mike. I'm scared for you, baby. Please be careful."

"All-fuckin- right! He thinks this a game? Mike's a dead muthafucka! He robbed our workers of what…? Thousands of dollars worth of product, and he thinks it's going down like that…? His ass is dead and stinkin!"

Black Rob was yelling loudly to Stack Money and Pretty

Boy as if they were deaf. The trio continued walking through the projects with revenge clouding their path.

"A yo Rob, I've been down with Mike for a long time. I'm not too sure that I'm down with killing him over some money," added Stack Money.

He saw what look like a shadow behind the building they stood in front of.

"Listen up, niggas… Listen real good… I love this coke and dope game. This is real paper. Shit! For the first time, we getting' real money… I'll be damned if Mike or his bitch's gonna stop my cash flow. He violated and is fuckin' slowin' down my paper. He thinks I'm playin'? His ass is dead and stinkin!" screamed Rob at his boys.

Coming out of the shadows, behind the building was Old School with his guns at the ready. Mike had dropped him off and Old School went looking for Black Rob. After eavesdropping on their plot, Old School now knew Black Rob's intentions. He came out of the shadows.

"Who's dead Nigger? I know you ain't threatening my boy's life over no lost drug money. Now you all grown up and tasted some long paper, you wanna kill the same man that bought your pun- ass out of the house to get dough. What's up with that Rob?"

Rob saw the guns in Old School's hands and started stuttering while falling back.

"Yo… yo-yo… Old School. I-I ain't got no beef ain't wi-with you. It's Mike. Tell him to leave my workers and product alone and we won't have any problems," said a nervous Rob.

"Nah, you can tell him yourself. Let's all walk over to my truck real easy, and we can meet up with Mike. Then we can see what he thinks about all these threats on his life."

Old School lost sight of Stack Money. He turned to feel the blow of a hard object colliding with the side of his head. He fell and his head hit the floor.

"Hurry up slowpoke. You always have to take twenty-two hours to get ready," Mike impatiently yelled at Laura.

They were already late for a party at the Savoy Manor, being held in honor of a childhood friend. He had just gotten released from jail after serving ten years, and they were going to celebrate his release.

"If your horny ass could go one day without sex, maybe we would be on time. You expect to just run up inside me, and then I'm suppose to go to the party with you dripping down my leg, and my hair busted, not," said Laura, lashing right back at Mike. "Anyway, I'm ready. Let's go."

"You look beautiful tonight, baby. I love what you're wearing," complimented Mike.

"Thanks handsome, you look kinda fly yourself..."

Mike and Laura were driving in their BMW to the dance, but couldn't take their eyes off each other. If they had paid more attention to the road and their surroundings, they would've realized they were being followed since leaving home.

"Baby, you know I've been thinking. Let's forget about that six months timetable and get out of the game right now. We have a pretty decent stash. Let's go down south and start a business. Have a family, like we always talked about," pleaded Laura, getting an uneasy feeling.

"It's like you can read my mind. I'm tired of all this shit that's going on. Besides I don't want to go to war with Rob and my boys over some damn drug money, or anything else for that matter. Tomorrow we'll meet up with School and tell him we're out of the game, and then we can be off to do us. Okay boo?"

"That's perfect, my baby. I love you so much Michael."

At the stoplight, the couple hugged. They were three blocks away from the Savoy. A black Caravan with tinted windows pulled alongside the preoccupied couple's car. They were caught up in each other's splendor and paid no attention. Suddenly the sliding doors rapidly opened. Fire sparked from the interior of the vehicle. There were no more sounds.

Chapter 04

"Fuck I'm— Oh I'm... I'm ah...coming. Oh shit! Goddamn baby! That was really un-fuckin-believable. I've never in my life come so many times and so intensely. What time is it anyway?"

Laura glanced at the clock. It was eleven in the morning. She freaked out.

"I can't believe we've been at this non-stop for all these hours. How in the hell do you keep going so long? What the hell have you turned into a robot?" said a trembling Laura to her energized lover.

"Baby, I don't know but I just couldn't stop. And my shit is still rock hard."

The couple couldn't remember arriving at the apartment

after the party at the Savoy or how they ended up in this sex marathon, but the lovemaking was totally out of this world.

"Laura baby, we have to get out of bed sometime and go tie up some loose ends before we leave," said Mike, stroking his shaft.

"Okay Mike, but can't we get something to eat first? I'm starving. Baby, bring me some water, please."

After bringing Laura a glass of water, Mike walked into the bathroom to take a shower. She heard him shouting, "Laura what's wrong with this shower knob? It ain't working."

"Don't be so impatient boo just take your time and the knob will turn," said Laura, joining him.

The water came on with Mike's hand still on the knob. The couple took a quick bath together. Feeling famished, they raided the refrigerator.

"Wow! I've never been this hungry before. Are you ready to go yet?" asked Mike buttoning his shirt.

"In a second baby I'm just listening to Roger and Sandra argue about some woman that he got caught creeping with," answered Laura, her ear pressed against the front door.

"Excuse me, but what are you doing? Sandra lives five flights beneath us. How the hell...? Wait a minute, I hear 'em too. Damn, they must be really going at it for us to hear them all the way up here, huh?"

"Pretty Boy, we better go check on Old School and make sure he's still alive. That head blow put him out," said a nervous Stack Money.

Pretty Boy walked a few steps ahead of Stack Money. They entered a house cross-town. Stack Money had blindsided Old School, they had tied him up and kept him in the basement of a rented house used for stashing drugs. While walking down the stairs leading to the basement, they noticed a window to the backyard was smashed and the chair Old School was tied in was empty.

"Today is gonna be a hot one baby. Can we stop in the park before we go take care of business?" Laura asked her man.

"No problem, baby. You know I love showing off the finest woman in the city."

"Save the sweet talk. No more pussy for awhile, my shit is on fire for real."

Mike and Laura walked into their favorite park. A sleeping pit bull lying under a tree was suddenly awakened and started barking viciously. The dog charged full speed toward the couple suddenly the animal stopped several feet in front of them. Then the dog turned and ran out of the park leaving his owner dumbfounded.

"Crazy ass mutt, let's be out boo. There's no sense in putting this off any longer," said Mike.

They held hands as they walked out of the park. The sights greeting them when they strolled in the hood were confusing to Mike.

"Can you believe this? These niggas still out here slinging poison… This has got to stop."

Mike and Laura arrived in the projects. Mike started walking toward a group of Pretty Boy's workers, but Laura stopped him.

"Michael, are you crazy? How are you gonna rush these young thugs for their drugs without Old School or your gat? You buggin', baby…"

"Oh shit you right, ma. I still wanna holla at them real quick like. No beef." Walking to the crew of boys, Mike started talking loudly. "Yo my brothers, this shit you selling is killing our people, don't that bother ya'll?"

It seemed the young hustlers were ignoring Mike. Then one of them said, "I ain't tryin' a hear that mess. I'm gonna go check my girl. I'll holla at you cats."

"We almost finished anyway. Let's be out. We can stop by Cozy and get some herb," a tall, skinny dealer suggested.

"Word, it's getting slow out here anyway," said another dealer.

Watching them walk away peacefully brought a smile to Laura's face. She walked to where Mike was standing.

"Baby, what did you say to them?" she asked.

"I really don't know. I guess they were showing me some type of respect by leaving the set."

"See no matter what, you still the man, Mike," said Laura, gassing up her man.

The couple walked a while longer through the projects. They observed all the things that were still out of control. Everyone seemed to be ignoring them and went about their lives. Laura started getting nervous.

"Baby, I think we're pressing our luck out here, someone is bound to recognize us and holla at Black Rob, and we out here unprotected."

"Okay, let's swing by School's house, and see what he found out about Rob's next move."

"What's up with this bell? It's busted. Yo School it's me playa open up," shouted Mike. He was standing in front of Old School's house while Laura waited on the curb.

"Baby, let's go around the back. School might be sleeping or in the shower, his truck is in the driveway," said Laura.

The two walked around the side of the house to the backyard. They looked through a window and saw Old School sitting on the couch. He had a bandage around his head and was talking on the phone.

"What you mean you think he did it... Did what?" School stood up and looked toward the back of the house while he waited for the other party to respond. He appeared really nervous and jittery. "Yeah, yeah, I'm still here. I just felt... Never mind. So they're not at their house and he's bragging that he runs shit now. So what are you saying?" There was a pause from Old School. "Oh hell no...! I can't believe that shit. No fuckin' way!" Old School dropped the phone.

He ran toward the front door. Mike and Laura yelled out his name. It seemed that Old School paused a second before walking quickly out the door. Mike and Laura ran around to the front of the house to see Old School's truck immediately screeching out the driveway.

"Yo School, Old School, hold up you deaf bastard! It's your boy Mike," shouted Mike at the top of his lungs.

"That nigga must have his music on full blast," said Laura, holding Mike's hand.

"Damn! We just missed him. I needed to holla at Old School today, baby. I wanna find out what the hell is going on in these streets."

"We'll catch him. But for now can a sister get a meal and something to drink? I'm starving."

"Sure cutie, actually I'm starving myself. It's crazy, but lately I can't get enough to eat or drink. It's some bugged out shit for real," replied Mike.

Hand in hand, Mike and Laura walked down the street, enjoying each other's company.

"Is it me, Mike? Or do things seem a little strange to you, baby?"

"Nah baby, it's not just you. I've been feeling a little awkward myself. It's probably all the drama. You know… Maybe the anxiety about leaving the game got us buggin'… Let's just go home. I think another fuck marathon is what the doctor ordered."

"You're so ill, baby. Where do you get the energy? Mike, just please, this go round don't be shifting around my damn organs, okay?" pleaded Laura.

"Okay, I promise, just your pancreas."

They both started laughing and just walked hand in hand enjoying the warm summer's night air.

Chapter 05

Laura and Mike walked the streets for several hours talking about life and their love for each other. They planned about moving away from the city, and starting their own family.

"I want one boy and a girl," Laura said.

"I want my own football team worth of kids," Mike joked.

The couple walked and talked until finally they wound up in their favorite park. They sat on their favorite bench, making out like horny teens. Suddenly, a cool breeze came out of nowhere and sent a chill through their bodies. Mike took off his New York Knicks jersey. He put it on Laura, leaving him wearing a wife beater.

"Thanks baby, you're always so considerate, but you might catch a cold," Laura said, looking off into the distance. "Now baby, what's that cat's story?"

Laura pointed to the trees, and Mike looked. He saw a strange looking man who was dressed like he was going to a ball, or a funeral. He had on an ancient three-piece suit that was a blend of white and black. What was even more peculiar about this old fashion dude was that the couple couldn't make out his face clearly. It seemed like he was shrouded in a shadow. Even as he moved through the trees watching the couple watch him, he was always engulfed in a fog-like covering.

"He looks like he should be on the late, late, late show hanging out with Boris Karloff and some mummies, for real," joked Mike.

The strange figure disappeared behind the bushes.

"Baby, you're so silly," said Laura laughing. "But you're right, he did look mad creepy."

The couple cuddled and watched some kids at play by the lake. Laura suddenly let a scream and started shivering. Mike immediately grabbed her cold, goose-pimpled hand and asked, "What's wrong baby?"

"Oh baby, I was just staring out at the water and suddenly I had a vision of lakes of fire and people in chains crying out in agony and drowning in pools of blood. It only lasted a few seconds, but it felt so real," said the still shivering Laura.

"Okay, lakes of fire and pools of blood… Hmm you know Laura, I use to see that same image back in the days every time I smoked a bag of that red devil angel dust," Mike said, laughing and being his normal sarcastic self.

"You don't believe me. Well thanks a lot funny man. I know I wasn't bugging out, Mike."

"I know, baby. I'm just teasing you, cutie. It's probably you're just reacting badly to all that's been going on lately. Baby, on the real though, I had a crazy vision when we were making love last night. When I was on my back and you were acting like you were in a rodeo, I looked up and could've sworn I saw the faint shadow of a woman flying over our bed and smiling, bugged me out," said Mike, trying to laugh it off.

"Mike what's going on with us?"

"Nothing Laura, let's just go home baby, we probably just need to chill and get some rest that's all."

Mike and Laura returned home. Raiding the refrigerator, they again devoured the remainder of food and water left in the house. After eating, they went to bed to get some rest before attempting to locate Old School and tell him they were getting out of the game. Mike had fallen asleep before Laura and as she was about to doze off she was startled by Mike's screams.

"No Dad, come back. Don't leave me again, please dad come back."

Laura shook Mike until he started coming out of his dream.

"Baby wake up, you were having a bad dream."

Even though the room was very cool, Mike woke up

breathing hard and his body was soaked with perspiration. He got out of bed and went to the bathroom. He must have drunk a gallon of water from the faucet.

Mike returned to the bedroom looking at a worried Laura and said, "That was a crazy dream baby. You believe after all these years I dreamt about my father? Yo, I dreamed that he came into the bedroom and sat down by the bed, and baby, we laughed and talked for hours. He said he was sorry he left me so soon and that he loved me." Mike's eyes started to tear up. He caught himself and went on. "He was about to tell me sump'n. And suddenly he looked away, and then he got up, saying it was time for him to go. I reached out to grab him but felt nothing, and he just drifted away. Laura I don't know what he was trying to tell me, but as he was disappearing he said, 'Please my son choose wisely.'"

"Wow Mike, that was some damn dream, baby. You know in all these years I never heard you say that you dreamt about your dad once."

"That's what's so ill, baby. I just started thinking about him these last few days, and now I have this dream."

"Honey, I'm not gonna front, these last few days have been crazy strange, for real. Ever since we came back from the party at the Savoy I have been feeling real strange," said Laura.

She started shivering again and Mike wrapped a blanket around both of them.

"Laura, you know what's also strange now that you mention

the party? I can't remember shit about what happened that night. We must have been bent, because that entire night is a blank."

"Mike you know that's true baby. I can't recall the party at all… Not getting there or leaving. I do remember that you were looking extra fine that evening, and I wanted to pull over and get busy in the car."

"She's a very freaky girl," Mike started singing while rubbing Laura's shapely legs.

"No wait baby," Laura suddenly yelled, pushing Mike's hand from between her thighs. "I think I remember us driving down Jerome Avenue and we were talking and laughing, but after that everything is a blank," exclaimed a troubled Laura.

The couple sat in the bed, lost in their thoughts for a few minutes. Then it was as if something just seemed to pop in Mike's head he said, "Boo, do you remember hearing shots that night?" Mike asked, standing up.

"No… Not really. I think I remember hearing some clapping noises like fire crackers but I don't think they were gunshots."

"Let's not bug out about it Laura. That night is a total blur. I guess it will come back to us eventually. Let's get dressed and hit the streets, maybe we can go by the stash house and find School and get some answers, okay?"

"Sure lover, let's be out. We really need some answers and hopefully closure to all this mess."

Mike started walking to the door and Laura grabbed him.

"Before we go lover I have a slight problem I think you can help me with. It seems that my ovaries are a bit dry. Do you know where I could get some lubrication?" Laura said while grabbing the front of Mike's pants.

"I just happen to have a portable lubricator right where your hand is," said Mike smiling. "But your tonsils look a little dry also. So first things first, open up and say Ah!"

Chapter 06

"Mike this has to be the craziest idea you've ever had. It will never work. We look like two deranged crack-heads," said Laura, referring to the way they were dressed.

Mike had the idea of going undercover in the projects. He was still trying to find out any information about Black Rob's new operations and the plans for retaliation against Mike. They had been looking for Old School to get answers for several days now, but with no luck. Mike and Laura were tired of the anticipation and wanted to put an end to the ordeal.

"Damn girl, even as a crack-head you still look fine," said Mike.

He was dressed in a torn coat and busted shoes. Laura smiled looking at him.

"Well I don't feel fine. This is crazy, Mike and it won't work. Someone is bound to recognize us," complained Laura ripping a hole in her stockings.

"Okay Scotty, let's go fight those Klingons," laughed Mike.

He left the apartment with a furious Laura lagging behind. Disguised in their rundown drug addicts' attires, Mike and Laura went into the projects. Business was going on as usual. There were crack and dope peddlers all through the projects. The couple overheard that the dealers were all claiming to be down with the Get Money Crew. This knowledge made Mike furious. He kept his head and continued to gather information. They decided to approach a group of hustlers who were in a heated discussion.

"Nigga you buggin'— the shit we got from Rob last time was much better than this weak-ass coke. I clocked my whole package in two days. This new shit is goin mad slow," shouted a tall, slender crack dealer.

"I know the heads in my building love this shit. And the bitches are freakin' hard for a blast of this butter," rebutted his dark skinned co-worker.

Their discussion went on for a few minutes. Mike decided to try and get some inside information. He approached the men and they walked away without paying him any attention. Laura walked up behind him saying, "I guess you overdid it Captain Kirk. They probably thought your dusty looking ass was dead broke."

"Don't give up your day job funny lady. Let's go," said Mike.

They walked through the projects trying to locate Old School, or any member of Mike's renegade crew. They were unsuccessful.

"What the hell, I know we look like shit and you smell pretty... Just joking baby, but why the hell is everyone just ignoring us, like our dough is monopoly money?" asked an upset and frustrated Laura.

Exhausted Mike and Laura sat on a bench. Mike pondered other possibilities while Laura pulled her shoes off and rubbed her tired feet.

"Maybe if you put your shoes back on people wouldn't be avoiding us like the damn plague," said Mike.

"If they smell so bad then why you love sucking them so much, along with the rest of my body?" said Laura, wiggling her toes in Mike's face.

Mike grabbed his stomach, and put his hand over his mouth, acting like he was about to vomit.

"You're so silly Michael, I swear."

Mike moved closer to Laura and started rubbing her feet. They were relaxing on the bench. While talking, Laura looked in the lobby of a building, and touched Mike's arm.

"Baby, isn't that the same man we saw in the park the other day, wearing that same bugged out suit?"

Mike glanced over at the building and smiled then said, "Word baby. That's Boris, but why does he keep popping up in the weirdest places, and what's the story with that suit? I think I'm gonna go check out homeboy real quick."

The couple started walking toward the building, and a group of kids came running out of the door. Mike and Laura moved out the way to let them pass.

"Oh shit, where did he go so fast?" asked Mike, entering the lobby.

Mike and Laura stood in the lobby talking. Two men exited the elevator also in conversation, and what they said caught the couple's attention.

"Yeah man, that cat Stack Money got his wig peeled back. He got shot three times in the face," said one of the men.

"Word, do they know who did it?"

"Not really, but cats are saying it was Old School, on some payback shit."

The two men left the building oblivious to the couple in the corner. Laura looked at Mike digesting what they just heard.

"That's bullshit. Old School wouldn't kill Stacks, and what payback shit? The two of them were cooler than a fan."

"I don't know Mike. That might explain why we can't find School anywhere. It might sound crazy, but the way shit is going on these days crazy is in season," added Laura.

They quickly walked out the projects and heading home.

"What the fuck? Laura, we been robbed!" shouted Mike, walking into the apartment.

The front door was slightly ajar. The place had been cleaned out, not ransacked, but neatly emptied. The couple looked through the entire apartment and found everything missing including their clothes.

"Ah hell no…! This is crazy, all our shit is gone. Every piece of furniture and our gear…" Mike was at loss for words.

"Baby, they even took out the phone. I better go to one of the neighbor's and call the police," suggested Laura.

They both decided to go together, but only to return moments later with a look of surprise written on both their faces.

"You mean to tell me in this entire building not one person is home. What's up with this fuckin' twilight zone shit, baby?"

"Mike, I'm getting really freaked out about what's been happening lately. None of this is making much sense. The more answers we look for, the more questions pop up."

The two hugged each other in a tight embrace and started thinking about the events of the last few days. Everything that had been happening kept bringing them to one troubling question. Suddenly the lovers separated and looked at each other. Like always, they were reading each other's mind.

"What happened that night?" They both chorused.

Chapter 07

During the weeks that followed, members of the renegade Get Money Crew, now led by Black Rob and Pretty Boy, turned the southeast section of the Bronx into a drug-infested ghetto. With the various projects in the area flooded with heroin and crack, new addicts were being recruited every day.

The surge of strung out crack-heads and junkies also brought a wave of crime and violence. Robberies and break-ins were at all time highs. Women and men who once worked to support families now turned to prostitution to support there out of control drug habits.

Mike and Laura had been staying in their apartment for some time now. They stopped going into the projects and gave up trying to locate Old School. They didn't want to push their luck and be recognized.

"This is getting out of hand, baby. Those greedy bastards have turned our hood upside down. People we grew up with are fucking with that poison and throwing their lives away," said Mike looking out the window at a crack-head breaking into an automobile. "Laura we both know that drugs always been in the projects, but not like this. It looks like a damn epidemic."

Mike and Laura left the apartment to walk to the store. The two had been living on fruits and water that they stole from the neighborhood Korean fruit stand. Their bankcards wouldn't work after they were robbed of their valuables and cash. They went by their relatives' homes to collect other stashed monies, but nobody was ever home. With all the strange events happening, the couple mostly stayed home talking, and making love. Sitting on a car drinking water and eating fruit Laura and Mike discussed their misfortunes.

"This can't last forever baby. As soon as we straighten out these streets and get a hold of our people to get our money, we're history, no looking back," promised Mike.

Laura eyed him and ate her banana. As they went walking down the street they saw Carl, one of Rob's main workers coming their way with one of his girls. The couple ducked into a doorway acting like they were looking for their keys. Carl and his girlfriend walked by Laura and Mike, they were having an interesting conversation.

"No, you can't come with me tonight, this is business. I gotta meet Rob and his connect later tonight at the Savoy. Listen baby, it's a private meeting we're having. No chicks allowed," Carl told his suspicious girlfriend.

"You just better not be bringing one of your bitches there with you Carl."

Carl started laughing and put his arm around her waist. They crossed the street.

"Baby, you think it's a good idea to just show up at the Savoy like this? We don't know what Rob is up to, or if he's still mad at you and School for robbing his workers."

"We'll know soon. We're almost there. Then we'll find out where we stand with Black Rob and his new Get Money Crew."

The couple began walking to the Savoy, which was not far from the apartment. Mike started feeling strange.

"Wow Laura, you feel how cold it got all of a sudden. And what's up with that smell?"

Laura buttoned up her sweater, and looked around to see if she could find the source of the decomposing smell. She glanced across the street. Standing in a lighted doorway was that same suited stranger. He was staring down an alley on their side of the street.

"Oh, now look at this, not again. Why does this nut-job keep on popping up all the time?" Laura asked. She noticed that Mike was looking down the same alley the strange man was looking. He was in a trancelike state. "Baby what's wrong?" asked Laura, hugging Mike.

"Baby, I got a weird feeling that something down that alley will answer some of the questions about these strange things that's been happening to us lately. Whatever stinks like that is down there."

"Baby, I'm scared. Let's just go," said Laura.

Mike started walking down the alley. Laura followed her man. They ventured deeper into the alley and Laura felt that something was pulling them. Suddenly there was a dead end. Nothing but a dumpster was standing between them and a brick wall. Trash was overflowing because of the still unresolved sanitation strike. The origin of the smell was in front of them. They knew this wasn't the smell of garbage or urine.

Something was sticking out from the back of the dumpster. Mike glanced at Laura first before moving closer to get a better look. Laura looked at Mike. She saw utter terror and fear on his face. Without asking him a thing, she also took a look.

What Laura saw made her scream in a blood-chillingly, loud way. The couple was looking at the decomposing bodies of a man and woman that were riddled with bullet holes. Laura screamed, not because she saw two dead bodies, she had seen death before. Laura and Mike were looking at their own rotting flesh lying there lifeless. The couple walked out of the alley in a state of shock and disbelief.

"How can that be us, baby...? We're right here, alive and kicking," said Mike, holding Laura close and looking into her eyes. "We're here baby, but are we alive?"

The couple started discussing all the strange and weird things that had been happening since that night of the party. Slowly, everything started to make sense. They never got to the party that night. Now they knew why everyone ignored them when they came around. Their house was emptied and none of their relatives ever answered when they went knocking.

Everything made sense, except if they were dead, why were they still here in spirit?

Mike and Laura tried to answer that last crucial question but couldn't. Then they looked at each other and knew who would have the answer— the stranger. They looked across the street and he was there looking at them.

Chapter 08

"Shit! I thought you were horny when you were alive. Damn! If I knew the sex would be like this, I'd a killed your ass years ago," moaned Laura.

She had just finished having her eighth orgasm on the floor of the vacant apartment.

The place had been robbed by neighborhood crooks after learning of the couple's demise. Robbers staked out the place for days before having the courage to rob the apartment. The couple stayed there while they tried to make sense of their situation.

"You're right baby, the sex is bananas. And your coochie is crazy soft… Hmm," said Mike, licking his lips. Ah…Warm like an angel food cake... Get it?" laughed Mike, basking in a post-orgasmic huddle.

"Angel food cake, ha-ha very funny, but seriously boo— oh snap, get it, I said boo," said Laura, cracking up at her own joke.

"Yeah, yeah I get it, very funny, whoopee," laughed Mike sarcastically.

"Seriously Mike, what are we going to do? We have to get some answers. I don't think this is it."

Mike walked to the window and said, "Okay, this is the deal. That quack in the suit—he's tied into this somehow. I know it. We'll go out and get some answers one way or the other. Let's get dressed."

"Why are we getting dressed Mike? Nobody can see us," inquired Laura.

"For one, I ain't walking around with my jewels swinging in the breeze, and your coochie stays under wraps and covered up. That shit is so good it might start raising the dead."

"You're a sick puppy, Michael, but sweet... Let's get dressed."

The couple went out a few days before. Mike and Laura stole food and clothing from a few stores. They still couldn't understand why they were so hungry and thirsty even though they were dead.

Laura came out of the room in spandex biker shorts and a belly exposing T-shirt. Mike stared at her then started laughing.

"Baby, you crazy...? All these years you took pride in dressing conservatively, and now that you're dead you wanna be Caspisha, the ghetto-fabulous ghost," he said, giving Laura a kiss on the cheek. "Let's go, my little deceased hood-rat."

Laura laughed then punched Mike lovingly on his arm. Together they walked out of the apartment hand in hand.

"There he goes, Laura, walking to the park."

The couple had been searching for hours. While walking, they felt a cold breeze and Mike spotted the stranger. The couple ran in the man's direction and realized they were moving extremely fast.

When they reached the man, Mike tried to grab hold of him, but his hand seemed to bounce off the stranger's body. The stranger turned and smiled at the couple.

"I guess by now you know that you're not in the best of health."

Laura and Mike looked at each other furious. Mike again tried to lash out and grab the man. His hand just brushed off once again.

"Okay, I'm sorry. I know that you are confused and want answers. I know that you've figured out some of what happened to you. And yes, I have answers."

The three started walking through the park, talking. They sat on a park bench.

"Yes, you are here for a reason. You see your souls are in a state of limbo… A sort of stop over between the physical world and the hereafter," the stranger explained to them.

"Yeah, we figured that part out. But why us…? Can't we just get dirt thrown in our faces and move on like everybody else?" asked Laura with concern.

"Laura, I'm just a collector of souls, and occasionally a messenger. Believe me when I say you're not alone. Many before you have been faced with similar tests."

"What test?" interrupted Mike.

"Mike, you and Laura have unfinished business on earth before you can move on. The accomplishment of the business itself will determine your faith."

"Oh well, that explains everything. I'm so glad we had this little…"

Looking toward the entrance of the park, Mike stopped in mid-sentence. It was there he saw Black Rob parking his BMW. The same one he was driving the night he was murdered. All Mike saw was his murderer and the murderer of his beloved Laura, nothing else. He forgot all that the stranger had told him and started running at top speed toward Black Rob with murderous intentions in his heart.

Mike neared the exit to the park but he tripped and fell. When he finally got up what he saw filled his heart with terror. Instead of the park, or the street, Mike saw an endless lake of boiling oil. In the lake was a countless supply of phantom-like bodies all moaning and groaning. They were all climbing on top of each other in a concerted effort to not be submerged in the molten pit.

"Mike baby, are you ok?" asked Laura, catching up to her man.

"Yeah baby, I'm, I'm... What did I just see?" Mike asked the stranger who appeared next to Laura.

"Mike, you saw what might be waiting for you. Mike, Laura, you are being tested to see what's truly in your hearts. Your choices will determine your fate for eternity. Your lives were taken tragically by evil men. If you repay evil with evil," the stranger paused, looking at both their faces. "Then you better practice your lava backstroke…"

"Will you stop joking? This is our souls at stake here," screamed Laura in frustration.

"I'm sorry Laura. I truly feel your pain. I joke because your choices are so simple. But only you can make them."

Laura turned to Mike with tears in her eyes and said, "Mike, you're my love and I'm yours, let's just forget our anger and move on baby. I think we both know what our choice has to be. I want to walk through the Pearly Gates with you, and besides I can't swim for shit."

The couple turned to the stranger, who smiled then suddenly vanished.

"Mike, why did we walk this way?" asked Laura as they headed home to discuss the news the stranger gave them.

"I just wanted to see the old hood one last time, baby. That's all. We've lived here all our lives. Let's just say goodbye."

While walking through their old haunts, they went around a

corner that they have a thousand times before.

"Oh shit! There goes those murdering muthafuckas!" shouted Mike, referring to Black Rob and Pretty Boy. They were coming out of an apartment building. "I got something for..." Feeling a hand on his Mike turned to see Laura. Her tears melted Mike's heart, and his anger went too. He looked at his murderers again then at his woman. He held her and said, "Let's go, baby."

Chapter 09

"Ok we're ready anytime you are," shouted Mike.

He and Laura were sitting on their bench in their favorite park.

"Michael, stop that your ass is gonna get struck by lightning."

"But baby, the stranger said if we choose to forgive our killers that we would pass our test and move on, at least that's the way I read our conversation. We saw those bastards and just walked away. So why are we still among the living?"

"I don't know, baby. But there must be a reason," answered Laura.

"Laura, any more water in that bottle?"

"Yeah baby…"

Mike thought about the bottle at the end of the bench. It floated into his hand.

"Making things move is really cool, baby. Let me see if I can lift up your skirt."

The couple discovered advantages being among the half-dead. They possessed special gifts like being able to move extremely fast, and limited telepathic powers to move small objects. The best perk was being able to make love for hours, enjoying endless supply of orgasms.

"Listen horny man, stop playing. We have to find out what's left for us to do," said Laura, pulling down her skirt that was now floating around her waist.

"Baby I don't know what's left, but I know what I want to do."

"What Michael?"

"While we're still here let's put a little monkey wrench in Black Rob's organization. You down?"

"Let's do it baby," said Laura, looking at Mike and reading his thoughts.

Mike and Laura waded through the hood. Finally, they stopped at house used as a major stash spot for Black Rob's illegal drugs. At the back of the house, they looked through a window and saw what they were looking for.

In the house were ten totally naked women standing

around a table. They were all packaging coke and dope for Black Rob's enterprise. He had them working in the nude because he trusted nobody. It was a method of cutting down on drugs coming up short. Rob even had his workers' vaginas and anuses checked before they left the house, in case they had a coochie full of coke or a crack full of crack.

Laura noticed that the stove was on and all four burners were at full blast. She told Mike that a nice fire is what they needed. Mike saw that curtains were covering a window on the other side of the room. He tried to imagine moving the curtains to the stove, but couldn't.

"Come on Laura, concentrate with me, baby."

They began to think hard about moving the curtains. Mike started to chant softly.

"What the hell, are you some type of Tibetan monk? What's with the chanting? Just think harder, screwball," said Laura, laughing at her man.

"Okay, let's concentrate."

The curtains slowly started rising from the rods and hooks. Undetected the curtains slid along the ceiling.

"That's it baby, keep thinking."

Almost instantly flames leaped up as the curtains touched the stove.

"Oh shit! Fire! Fire! Let's get the hell out of here!" screamed a chick with a mound of bushy pubic hairs.

"What about the dope, Karen?" asked a petite black woman.

"Fuck that, I ain't burning up for another nigger's shit. I'm out."

The workers all ran out the door leading to the front of the house. One of the last women to leave took a large bag of coke and shoved it inside her vagina. She left wobbling.

"Oh fuck, Laura, did you see that chick? She must be fucking elephants, and donkeys, damn!"

Watching the dope go up in flames brought joy to the couple. They were relieved to see everyone made it out in time. For the next several hours they visited similar stash houses, and using different methods of their telepathic gift, they sabotaged nearly all of Black Rob's stash houses.

"That was fun baby. Well, I feel a lot better. We might never stop the drug dealings forever, but that should put a big dent in Rob's pockets."

Laura and Mike walked through the projects. They passed by Stack Money's building. The couple stopped dead in their tracks as they glanced by the benches in front of Stack's building. Walking around just in front of them looking crazed and confused, was Stack Money.

"Mike isn't that Stack? I thought those men said that he was dead."

"I don't know, baby. They said that Old School killed him on some payback shit. Maybe they heard wrong," replied Mike, looking baffled.

The couple stood there talking and heard laughter.

"Oh shit, so I really am dead, or can I see ghosts. What's up you two?" greeted Stack Money, walking over to Mike and Laura. He had a twisted and dangerous look on his face. "Boy you two look damn good for corpses," laughed Stack Money.

"You murdering muthafucka...!"

Mike was about to charge Stack Money, but Laura grabbed him by his arm and said, "Mike baby, no wait, we can't…"

Mike stopped and stared at Stack Money but stayed put.

"Ain't that a bitch? I kill you two, and badass Mike ain't gonna do shit. I see you still got your bitch running your show, nigga," said Stack Money. "Get this, I killed you two, and Old School killed me. You might not want your revenge but I damn sure am gonna get mine."

"Revenge for what?"

The three one-time friends turned around and saw the stranger sitting on a bench.

"Who the fuck is you?" inquired Stack Money.

"Let's just say that I'm your tour guide. Where you decide to vacation eternally is totally up to you."

"What the fuck is you talking about? Looking like a damn penguin in that suit and shit..."

"He's talking about eternity and choices Stack, yours and

ours. You killing School will only get you condemned to an eternity in the pit of hell. Let it go man, we have," said Mike trying to reason with his murderer.

Laughing hysterically, Stack Money angrily said, "Damn! You got it fucked up, baby-boy. School killed me because of you two. So before I get him, I got a score to settle with your asses. Far as that birthstone and fire shit, freeze that. I ain't having it!"

"Actually Mr. Stack, it's brimstone and fire," corrected the stranger.

"Yeah, brimstone this," Stack closed his eyes and pointed his hand at Laura and Mike.

"Stack Money think about what you're about to do. There's no second chance," warned the stranger, moving closer.

"Fuck that homey, Stacks don't forgive shit," said Stack Money.

Then he used the same powers Mike and Laura had to hurl objects at the couple. He threw garbage cans, benches, and anything that wasn't nailed down firmly, all came soaring in the direction of the unprotected couple.

Debris was hitting him, Mike looked over at Laura. She was ducking and dodging flying objects. Mike ran toward Stack Money, but before he got very far he heard Laura scream. He stopped cold in his tracks and turned to witness a pointed tree branch lodged in Laura's throat. She was gasping for breath. Mike ran over to her and held her. She looked into his eyes and he saw the light dimming in her eyes. He glanced at the stranger who was walking toward Stack Money.

"Laura baby, come on get up baby. How can you be hurt? We're already dead. This can't be happening."

Tears streamed down Mike's cheeks. Laura smiled at her life partner and whispered in his ears.

"It's okay, baby. It will only be for a short while. You'll be right behind me. Hurry up, boo," said Laura, vanishing.

Mike was left lying there, his outstretched hands were empty. The stranger walked over to him.

"But how…?" asked the shaken Mike.

Looking at Mike the stranger said sadly, "It's complicated Michael. You see, you, Laura and Stack Money are just partially dead. Living in a state of limbo amongst the living… Spirits in transition can actually harm each other. I'm sorry Mike, but believe me, Laura is in no pain. She passed her test and will be blessed with everlasting happiness."

Laughter came from the building as the stranger spoke to Mike. Mike turned to see Stack Money laughing.

"Oh Michael, I love you, it'll be okay," said Stack, mimicking Laura's last words.

Before the stranger could stop him, Mike ran over to Stack Money at super speed, thrusting his hand right through Stack Money's chest. Like a sword going through him, Stack Money heart went through his back.

"Ah, ugh, ah," murmured Stack, looking down at Mike's arm sticking out of his chest. "Damn Mike, I didn't think you still had it in you. Well player, looks like we both failed. See you downstairs, baby."

Stack Money fell to the ground, and his body absorbed into the earth. Mike stood there until a cool breeze hit him. The stranger stood by his side and looked at him with a disappointed stare.

"I know, I know, I fucked up. I just lost it man. Seeing my baby die in my arms was too much for me. I'm ready when you are, just make sure you take care of my boo."

Chapter 10

Mike and Laura knew what their choice had to be. If they chose wisely they would have been given a second chance in their afterlife. The couple's love and dedication for each other was so strong that even when facing their murderer, they chose to forgive them and save their immortal souls. An eternity of peace and loving each other was in their grasp, but then evil forces robbed them of their everlasting happiness. Or did it?

Losing his companion, Laura, and realizing that he was condemned to the hellfire, was enough to leave Mike walking the streets aimlessly. Lost in mournful thoughts, Mike walked and thought about his fate. A smile encompassed his face.

He knew that Laura, the only person on this planet that he truly worshipped, would not have to share his fate. Mike's wanderings brought him, not surprisingly back to the park. He sat on his and Laura's favorite bench. Mike leaned back and looked up into the sky.

"Baby, remember when we first met at the survivor seminar? Damn! I was hooked from the jump. I never told you this, but from that first moment I've been falling deeper and deeper in love with you every day of our life together. Sometimes when you're in bed asleep, I'd lay next to you wondering how I could possibly love someone so completely. There wasn't one moment in our lives together that I regretted being your man. You have made my life complete. I'll always be grateful to God for bringing us together. Baby, remember how we used to laugh together, cry together, love together and hell we even died together. Laura thank you for loving me so thoroughly," whispered Mike smiling. "I'm really gonna miss your sick sense of humor and that gorgeous smile. I'll especially miss that platinum pussy of yours. If you can hear me, I'll love you even after the sun burns out. If there's a way, I'll find you and we'll be together again. I promise my love."

Mike held his head down and felt a strong breeze blow by him. He looked around and saw nothing. Suddenly the stranger appeared next to him on the bench.

"Oh, what's up? I've kinda been expecting you. Thanks for everything, man. I know that you were rooting for us all along and I appreciate it. Word…"

The stranger turned around and Mike got a good look at his

face. There was a black eye on his mug.

"Damn! Who hit you player? I didn't know you angels got down like that," laughed Mike.

"We don't. It's your insane woman. She's going bananas upstairs. When she found out that you failed your test and wouldn't be joining her. Excuse my expression, but all hell broke loose."

"I hope you didn't hurt my woman, or I'll..."

"Hurt her? Look at me, man. She's decking everyone around her. Mike your woman loves you without reason, it's scary. Laura demanded to talk to the Father personally. She threatened to turn heaven upside down, and personally I believe she'd try."

"That's my girl, a real trooper. What will happen now?" asked Mike.

"Laura did have her one-on-one with The Boss. That has not happened since Moses climbed the rock. Anyway, she stated her case and it looks like you two will be together again."

"Word...? You mean the big man is gonna forgive me, and let me into heaven?"

The stranger then got up and walked a few feet before saying, "Not exactly Michael. You see Laura was ready to give up her place in heaven to join you in the pit."

"Hell no, that shit ain't gonna happen. My baby stays where she is. She deserves an eternity with nothing but happiness."

"That's just it Mike, Laura would rather die in the pit with you than live in heaven without you. Mike listen, the Father is harsh, but he's not blind. He knows what truly was in your heart. And at Laura's, request He has decided that the two of you will be together for eternity."

Mike started to smile but it was abruptly cut off by the stranger's next comment.

"But since you did kill in anger there must be some punishment. It has been decided that Laura will share your fate, and you'll share hers."

There was look of confusion on Mike's face as the stranger continued.

"Mike, you and Laura will spend half of a year in heaven, and the other half in hell, until the end of time. The love you two shared in life will echo into eternity. So let it be written… So let it be done. Mike you have been blessed with Laura and she with you. You two deserve each other. Take care."

The stranger vanished. The cool breeze that left with him was replaced by a cooler wind and a low hovering mist. Mike saw a figure emerge from the cloud. The figure drew closer and closer and smiled. The smile was Laura's.

Mike approached his love and she started speaking, "I leave you for one second, and you're down here doing open heart procedures… Getting condemned… What's up! Does someone need anger management classes?"

"Baby, it's really you," said Mike, embracing Laura. He refused to let her go.

Laura hugged her man tightly. She whispered in his ear, "Mike, I never want to be without you ever again. It's the worst feeling in the world," cried Laura.

"I know, but do you know what you gave up...? Why baby?"

"Why...? Michael, I love you. You're my life. What good is sitting on a cloud without you there rubbing my feet?" replied Mike's love.

"Damn! I love you."

"You better mister," said Laura, looking toward the horizon. "I guess we're off to see the Wizard," smiled Laura.

The couple gazed into each other's eyes and relished their embrace. They shared a passionately kiss until it was time to go. Spreading themselves upon on the wind, they grew thinner and thinner until only the rushing wind remained.

Epilogue

St. Raymond's Cemetery was a quaint little burial ground in the Throgs Neck section of the Bronx. The forecast for the Monday of the burial was rain and high winds. The meteorologist was very much on point. Wind howled through the trees and heavy rain soaked the ground.

One day after the sanitation strike was over a garbage man making a routine pickup discovered the bodies of Mike and Laura in an alley. After the families identified the bodies, they agreed on St. Raymond's because that was where both Laura's mother and Mike's father were buried.

The memorial service was held the Friday before the burial, and it was a sight to behold. Hundreds of men, women and children from the neighboring projects and communities came out to pay their last respect to the couple. Mike and Laura may have run a marijuana organization, but they used much of their profits to do a lot of charity work for the various communities in their region of the Bronx. Even the minister said they were truly a couple that gave back to their community and people. With rain coming down heavy, the last of the mourners were getting ready to leave the burial site. About two hours after the funeral was over an old friend stood over the gravesite to say goodbye.

"Sorry I got here so late. But I'm sure you know why I have to lay low. I've been out of town for a while now but I read about the funeral in the papers and well... Guys I'm so sorry that I couldn't stop what happened. You're my family and I should have been able to..." Stopping to regain his composure, the visitor continued. "Anyway, I just stopped by to tell you the old neighborhood is changing back to how it used to be. Black Rob's weak ass couldn't run shit without his flunkies. Pretty Boy got busted and Rob eventually started using his own product. You two should see him now all strung out and homeless. I saw him last night as I drove through. I was gonna rock his ass to sleep, but I figured drugs was already doing the job. I miss y'all a lot, man." Pausing for a moment, their friend continued. "Well boss and boss lady, be cool up there. I'll never forget you. Peace..."

Before leaving, the visitor looked at the headstone that rested on top of the remains of his lifelong friends and read the inscription.

"They shared everything in life and it's only right that they share their eternal resting place. Rest well Mike and Laura."

The stranger looked to see if anyone was nearby. He took out a knife from his pocket and bent down. Carving an inscription at the bottom of the headstone that read, "Thanks for being my friends your boy O.S."

Trees were rustling and the wind kicked up when the visitor stood up and started to walk away. The cemetery became suddenly cooler.

Old School stopped walking. He turned to look at the grave one last time. Perched on top of the headstone were two identical white doves. The birds looked at the visitor and cooed softly. Side by side they suddenly flew away into the horizon. Old School watched them and smiled. Just before they flew out of sight, Old School waved at them and said, "Later."

DEAD AND STINKIN'

HELL COMIN'
FROM HARLEM

Chapter 01

The entire wedding party was on time and the atmosphere was very festive. The only participants that were running late seemed to be the bride and groom. Malik, the groom was late because he was finishing up some last minute business that could not wait. Elaine, the future bride, did not have any excuse for her lateness.

"Malik, Elaine just got here and her bridesmaids are getting her ready. How you feel, player?" Big-O, one of the groomsmen asked, helping Malik with his jacket.

"I'm crazy nervous, man. It's not every day a cat like me marries a chick as fine as Elaine," the perspiring groom answered.

"Yeah, she's fine as hell, can't take that from her," AG said.

There to participate and share his special day were AG, Big-O, Hill, and Nes all childhood friends of the groom.

"Malik, it's almost time, you sure you want to go through with this?"

"What up with you, Hill? He's nervous already. You buggin' asking him that bullshit," Nes said.

Everyone knew that Hill never really liked Elaine for Malik. Hill used every occasion to constantly remind the crew of his feelings.

"Listen, Hill and the rest of you. I know how you all really feel about Elaine, but a cat like me loves that girl, y'all feeling me? Elaine's gonna be my bride, okay? Just get use to it, is all I'm saying. Now let's do this," Malik said.

"Okay, let's roll out," AG said, opening the door leading to the wedding chapel.

The wedding party all took their assigned places and the minister signaled the organ player to start the procession song.

All eyes were on the glowing beauty of Elaine. Time seemed stand still when she and her uncle came walking down the aisle. Elaine and her uncle took their positions. Then Malik started his journey down the aisle. The traditional order was switched at Elaine's request.

His eyes made contact with Elaine, and suddenly Malik felt like he was falling in love with her all over again. Thoughts of how they first met had him drifting halfway down the aisle. Malik smile widened like he was the luckiest man on earth. He was caught up in rapture, remembering that fateful night. It was Hill's birthday. Big-O, Malik, and AG were taking him out to celebrate.

"There it is, coming up on the right. Oh shit, it's on tonight," shouted Big-O in AG's ear.

He was pointing at the Golden Lady gentlemen's club. A popular strip club in the Bronx, and a special event was happening tonight. The crew parked the Benz and walked to the front entrance. They saw a group of half-naked dancers heading inside the club.

"Oh shit, look at them joints, it's on," shouted Big-O, grabbing his groin.

When the fellas entered the dark, smoky club, they were instantly rushed by a group of money-hungry strippers. Sensing that this was a crew of ballers, the strippers attacked them like hungry piranhas.

Malik, Hill, Big-O, AG and Nes all grew up together in Harlem and each man had his own drug organization in different parts of the city. Once a month they would hangout. Tonight all the friends were in the strip joint with the exception of Nes. His woman went into labor earlier that evening, and he was at the hospital expecting his first child.

"Can I have this dance handsome?" a tall, big-butt, bowlegged stripper asked Malik.

"No thanks. A cat like me is just here to celebrate my boy's birthday. Take him in the back room and take care of him, here,"

Malik said, peeling off dollars from a coil of bills.

He gave two one hundred bills to the wide-eyed chick. The dancer grabbed Hill by his waist and led him to a back private room.

"Yo Malik, what's up, man? A place full of ass in your face, and you acting like you scared?" Big-O laughed at his boy.

"Nah man, a cat like me is just..."

"Can I have this dance?"

Big-O and Malik turned to see who had interrupted their conversation. What they saw made them smile. Standing in front of them was a gorgeous woman with a body that was built like an Amazon warrior. When she spoke she had an erotic whisper, and dimples you could drink champagne out of.

"Hey handsome, can I...?"

Malik was caught off guard and looked dumbfounded at Big-O. Who was quick to respond, "Don't look at me, she's talking to you."

"My name is Chocolate," the dancer said, taking Malik by the hand. "What's yours?' she asked whispering in his ears and sending chills throughout his entire frame.

"Malik," he said, answering too quickly.

"Hmm... The strong type," she smiled.

Princess led him to the back room and the rest of the crew joined Big-O at a table.

"Damn, that bitch with Malik is fine! I know he's gonna trick all that paper on her fat ass, watch," A.G. said.

"Yo birthday boy, how was she?" Big-O asked Hill, ordering another round.

"What! She was bananas! I got a round-the-world special. She's a crazy freak."

"Don't tell me she gave you a batty-wash," laughed Big-O, taking a sip of his rum and coke.

"Shit, I got a wash, rinse and floss. Plus she got a set of twins of mine swimming in her stomach."

The three men shared the laugh. They were momentarily distracted by a lesbian freak show on the stage.

"Where the hell is Malik?" asked AG, nervously glancing at his watch.

"I don't know. He must be blowing that chick's back out after all this time."

"Oh, here he comes now."

Malik came walking through the front door, Chocolate clinging to his arm.

"Y'all cats still here. Me and Chocolate went to get a bite to eat. Now we're heading to the tellie and talk about it."

"Enjoy baby boy. I know I would," said Big-O with envy.

That night the crew went their separate ways after they left the club. The fun they had on their erotic excursion was all they were thinking about.

"Damn Malik, you've been seeing that stripper every single day this month. Her pussy sure 'nuff got you trippin', money," said AG, laughing at his friend.

The crew was busy playing basketball at the Polo Grounds Park, in Harlem. AG attempted another shot and it clanged off the front of the rim. Malik reached for the rebound.

"Chill with that yang, AG. I'm feeling Elaine. She's mad cool," said Malik.

"Elaine! Oh shit, what happened to Chocolate?" Getting serious A.G. continued. "Yo, Malik, don't forget where you met her at man. She's a ho', a stripper who fucks with ballers for their dough, that's her hustle. Don't let her hustle you. She may leave your ass dead and stinkin, home boy."

Nes, Big-O, and Hill looked at Malik. There was no denying that he was wearing the expression of a pussy-whipped man. The friends continued playing ball, and after they had ran two more games, they left the court. Returning to their separate drug blocks, they went back to take care of their illicit businesses.

All the warnings given to Malik by his crew didn't do anything to stop him from dating Elaine AKA Chocolate. He spent thousands of dollars on her and she got it in with passion for some of his paper. In a hot minute, Malik was head over heels in love. He made Elaine his number one and anointed her with a five caret diamond engagement ring.

That was two months ago. Now here he was walking down the aisle, getting ready to marry the woman of his dreams.

"I do…" Malik heard the words tumbling out of his mouth.

"I now pronounce you, man and wife," the preacher quickly added.

Malik and Elaine had officially tied the knot. They walked arm in arm out the church. He was wearing a white tuxedo complete with a proud smile. The bride and her bridesmaids wore white Vera Wang gowns. Even the veils could not hide the acid grin adorning all their faces. It was apparent that he was the only one feeling like he was in heaven.

"This reception is off the chain. They got some bad ass bitches up in da place. Elaine got some dime-piece friends. I'm talkin' 'bout-they-biz chicks, even if they all hookers," slurred a drunken Nes.

The friends stood around drinking and scanning the entire ballroom, admiring beautiful asses. Then they spotted an unexpected and unwanted guest.

"What's Rishon doing here? Who invited him?" they chorused.

"I don't know, but he's here, and watch how hard these chicks sweatin' him."

AG, Nes, and Hill just witnessed Rishon, a rival drug dealer, walking through the room. All of a sudden Malik appeared.

"Why y'all over here when all these fine single women are just dying to get with fly ass ballers, like all of you? What's up?"

"Rishon just walk up in here," said AG to Malik.

"I know Elaine invited that cat. That's her baby's daddy and they're still good friends. I ain't trippin."

The crew continued to keep their eyes on Rishon. Elaine came out of the back room with two of her bridesmaids. She spotted Rishon and immediately she beamed. Rishon walked over to her and kissed her on the cheek while whispering into her ear.

"Friends…? They look like more than just friends to me. Ah but what do I know?" observed Hill.

"What do cats like you know about anything but gettin paper? Leave it alone, I trust my wife, Hill," said Malik with a fake grin.

Malik looked on in disgust as Rishon and Elaine danced several songs. They seemed to fit each other easily in a way he wished he could, but he couldn't. Malik wanted badly to believe in her, but the way Rishon held her made him wonder.

After the fiasco at the reception, the couple left quickly. They immediately boarded a flight to Hawaii for their honeymoon, and stayed at the all exclusive hotel Renew in Honolulu.

"Baby, what's wrong?" asked Elaine, crawling into bed next

to Malik.

"What's wrong? You played me at the reception dancing with Rishon so damn long! My niggas were snapping on me all night," a lovesick Malik pouted.

"Sweetheart, he's my son's dad. And besides, your niggas are just jealous that you got me all to yourself, and they got nobody all to themselves."

"Yeah, but them cats..."

Cutting Malik off in mid-sentence, Elaine went to work. She kissed him hard on the mouth to stop his next words. Sliding her hand down to his groin, she gently massaged his testicles while sucking his nipple. Malik's head fell back and his moaning let Elaine know the argument was over.

She was a pro at fucking. Elaine used both hands to caress Malik's nipples. Her head came down to met his erect penis. His entire shaft was down her throat. Moving her head up and down, she simultaneously licked his balls. Malik was totally overwhelmed. No woman had ever freaked him the way Elaine did. Caught in the ecstasy, he was totally in love.

Malik didn't know what was on Elaine's mind. All he felt was her tongue action on his erection. In the midst of Malik's mind-blowing oral sex experience, Elaine looked up into his face .She then pictured the face of the man she truly loved.

Chapter 02

It had been two months since the couple returned from their Hawaiian honeymoon. Malik and Elaine were still acting like any newlywed couple. Staying in bed talking about their future, discussing how many kids they would have, and making love the rest of time.

A week prior to getting hitched, Malik purchased a five-bedroom house in Westchester County and a canary yellow BMW for his bride-to-be. Malik spoiled his new bride rotten, showering her with expensive gifts in the short time that he had known her. Any other woman in the world would have felt blessed to have such a caring, and generous man. Elaine's heart was however, somewhere else. The marriage didn't stand a chance.

"Baby, come back to bed. I got something I need to share

with you," a horny Malik called out from the bedroom on the top floor of the mini-mansion. "Are you downstairs?" Malik got out of bed, and walked to his private bathroom to brush his teeth. When he came back out, he went to the stairs and said, "Oh, Elaine, I guess you want to play games. Well I'm down. I'm a beat that ass when I find you."

Malik thought that Elaine was downstairs cooking him breakfast. Then he remembered that she couldn't even boil eggs. He searched the entire house and became concerned. He remembered not searching her closet. Malik ran there, but found it empty. Where the hell could she be? He thought, walking slowly. "Enough is enough, Elaine. Stop playing now," Malik called out.

Malik closely examined the closet, and noticed that a lot of the clothes he bought for Elaine were missing along with a set of Louis Vuitton luggage. Ideas started streaming through his mind, and Malik started to panic. Where could his new bride have run off to without telling him? His concern slowly teemed to anger.

"I can't understand it, AG. I haven't heard anything in days," said Malik with deep concern in his voice.

He and his boys were sitting in the small mansion that Malik had bought for Elaine. They were sipping Yak and discussing his wife recent disappearance.

"I've been really worried that she's been kidnapped," said a shaken Malik.

The rest of the crew stared at Malik and saw him fighting back his tears.

"Are you sure she was kidnapped? Maybe she just went away on some urgent business," Nes said, watching his boy fall apart.

"No man, I know she was kidnapped. My man in the Bronx who was at the wedding swore he saw Elaine walking in the courtyard up in Stevenson Commons," insisted Malik.

"I know the Commons. I used to hit this little shorty up there. That place is bugged out. It's in the Soundview area and all gated in like a damn fortress," said Nes, shaking his head.

"Hold up. Ain't that where Rishon comes from?" asked Big-O, looking around the room.

"Word...! That's that cat's hood, and he got it on smash too, but why would Elaine be there?" inquired Hill.

"Rishon is her baby daddy and that cat still loves her. That cat snatched up my wife and is holding her in the Commons. I know it," said Malik, looking around to see if his words had the effect he wanted.

"How can you be so sure it was kidnapping and not mutual, playa?" asked Big-O, hitting a nerve with Malik.

"Listen I know what I know. The back window was smashed in the kitchen. That cat must have snatched her up while she was down here trying to fix me sump'n to eat," said Malik pointing to the kitchen area.

The rest of the crew looked at each other suspiciously. They were not totally buying Malik's story, but they did not disbelieve it either.

"So what you gonna do now?" inquired Nes.

"I'm gonna... No, we're gonna go uptown and get my wife outta there, and bring her back home. That's what we're getting ready to do."

"Hold up, Malik. What we got to do with your marital drama? And besides we don't really know if she was really kidnapped," argued a reluctant Big-O.

"He's right, Malik. If we just go up there on some gangster shit, them Bronx niggas are gonna defend their turf. I ain't down for no war if there's no paper involved," added AG.

"Oh, it's like that. Wait a minute all of you cats." Malik said, going upstairs to his wall safe.

He pulled out a crumpled, old piece of paper and, brought it back downstairs.

"Do any of you cats remember this?"

They all looked at the old document. Finally Big-O said, "Oh shit I remember that. Damn kid, you kept that all these years?"

They all looked on the paper and read the few scribbled lines that were written on it.

"I know where this is going, Malik. We made that promise as kids, man. We were barely out of pampers. Shit, it's written in crayon for Christ sakes," said AG with a grin.

"Yeah well, I see you brothers or I should say acquaintances weren't serious about this pact when we wrote and signed it. But I was dead serious," said Malik in a disappointed tone of voice.

"Let me see this again," said Nes, taking the paper and reading it out aloud. "'The uptown boys solemnly swear to have each other's back and to protect and defend each other even if it means risking our lives. If one of us ever needs the others we will be there by their side one-hundred percent, no questions asked.' Damn ya'll, we did say, write, and sign off on 'em words. I can't speak for nobody else but Nes and I don't go back on my word."

"That's my boy! Come on Nes, real niggas do real things. Me and you can handle this by ourselves. So let's ride," said Malik, hugging Nes.

They both began walking toward the back door, when Hill shouted, "And the Oscar goes to... Quit the dramatics, kid. We all know what we wrote, and swore to. And you know that we got your back. I just got a fucked up feeling about this, Malik."

"Why Hill? Is it because you ain't feeling my wife?"

"Malik, we go back to playing Skelzies, man. So you know we down for whatever. But this could get real ugly, playa. Just so you know that," warned Big-O, who was usually the level headed member of the crew.

"Yeah Big-O, I know. But I love her and would kill to get her back."

"Okay, then let's get out of this house and meet up at Mount Morris Park to plan our next move," suggested Nes, taking out his car keys.

Hill got on his cellphone and dialed a number, "Hello Pat...? What's up? It's me. Listen... Meet me at Mount Morris tonight at eight o'clock. I'll explain everything later. Peace."

Hill ended the call and noticed that all his boys were looking at him with confusion on their faces.

"What! Ya'll know Patrick. He's my boy. He got heart for this, trust me. I want him to roll with us."

The rest of the crew looked at each other and walked out the back door.

"Damn this dro is strong, AG. Where you cop it?" asked Big-O inhaling the strong weed.

"My man, Stevie-D from Mid-town sold me an ounce. I figured we needed to get our heads nice and mellow before rolling uptown."

The crew was waiting for Malik to meet with them. Malik had just gotten off the phone when he pulled up in his benz.

"My man uptown tells me he spotted Elaine again. She and Rishon were beefing in the courtyard of the commons. I knew that cat had my girl up there. We all ready?"

"Yeah playa, the trucks are loaded with ammo and we all recruited a few soldiers from our crews to roll with us. By the way, that's gonna cost some strong chips, Malik," said AG, rolling another blunt.

"I got this. Everyone gets paid out of my pockets. Your cats will all be taken care of, trust me. Now let's be out."

"Hold up. We got to wait for Patrick. He should be here any minute," Hill said.

"C'mon, where is your little...?"

"My little what…? Don't play yourself, Malik. That's my boy," Hill said, defending Patrick.

Sometime ago Hill met Patrick at a club. They have been hanging tough ever since even though it was rumored that Patrick was gay. No one in the crew could confirm the rumor, but they knew Hill and Patrick spent a lot of time together.

"There he goes now," smiled Hill as he saw his friend approach.

"Sorry I'm late. I had to turn back to get my lucky gun. I couldn't go to a gunfight without her," said Patrick, smiling at Hill.

"Okay, can we fucking leave now? I want to be in and out by tonight. Let's not drag this shit out too long. Movements…!"

The order was given by Malik and a convoy of trucks headed across the Willis Avenue Bridge, crossing into the Bronx. The mission was to bum-rush Stevenson Commons, rescue the kidnapped Elaine, and return her to her rightful place beside her husband.

Chapter 03

"What do you mean you ain't worried about Malik? Rishon, you should be. He ain't playing. I heard he's coming up here to get me," Elaine said, trying to warn her accused kidnapper.

"Fuck Malik, and his boys too. Let them step to their business. I got sumthin for their ass," boasted Rishon.

Elaine could hear the fear in his voice. Her friend Tanya called and told her about the rumors circulating around Harlem that Elaine was kidnapped. Malik was going crazy and was planning on doing something about it.

"I just hope you have a strong crew because Malik does. And I know how they get down when they have beef," Elaine said with a smile on her face relishing the possibility of a war being fought over her.

"Listen here. Those niggas ain't the only ones with a strong mob. I got this. My brothers and cousin are coming to help me defend mines."

Rishon did indeed attempt to recruit his family members. Because of his rep of being a selfish, money-hungry coward who started problems then relied on his family to bail him out, they were all reluctant. At first they told him he was on his own, but when they were told the beef was with Malik, they agreed.

At one point in his life, Malik was a notorious stickup kid. He once robbed several of Rishon's family members who were also drug dealers. Rishon told Elaine about his family, she stopped stressing about the potential war.

Rishon and Elaine were inside his apartment, talking when his brothers walked in. They were each carrying a duffel bag under their arms.

"Oh baby, these are my brothers. This is Cornelius and Heckie," said a confident Rishon.

"Hey Elaine, we heard a lot about you from Rishon. It's nice to finally meet you," said Cornelius.

"Likewise Cornelius…" her voice trailed.

She rushed by Cornelius. Elaine paused and took Heckie's hand and smiled, looking him up and down, she said, "So you're Heckie. I've heard a lot about you from some of my girlfriends. It's a pleasure to meet you."

Elaine held Heckie's hand in hers longer than was necessary.

Cornelius noticed they were looking deeply into each other's eyes. He looked over at Rishon to see if he saw, but Rishon was busy inspecting the contents of the duffel bags.

"Now that's what da fuck I'm talking about! Crazy heat… Did y'all bring some troops?"

Heckie heard his brother's voice. He seemed to shake off his trance, letting go of Elaine's hand.

"Man, we brought a few homies with us. It worked out good because they all had beef with Malik and were itching to roll. Our crew is tight and ready. I just hope your scared ass don't act up," Heckie laughed.

Rishon thought the comment was disrespectful and stared angrily at Heckie. Elaine was smiling.

"I was born ready. Let's get ready to give them a warm reception. What's up with big cuz?" Rishon asked Cornelius.

"He had to round up his crew. He'll be here."

"Alright cool. Now, let's talk strategy," said Rishon looking at Heckie.

Heckie nodded his head in Elaine's direction. Rishon immediately caught on.

"Elaine baby, this ain't for you. Go downstairs to my mom's crib until I call for you," said Rishon kissing Elaine while walking her to the door. Rishon opened the door, and saw Sandra, his sister. She came barging into the apartment looking really upset.

"What's up ya'll? I hear you got some beef over a chick

and I had to see who the hell was worth all this drama..." Sandra caught sight of Elaine and shaking her head continued. "Ah hell fucking no…! I know you niggas ain't about to go to war over that ho'Chocolate."

Silence filled the room for the next few moments. Everyone just stood motionless. Elaine shot daggers at Sandra. Ferociously rolling her eyes, Elaine stomped out the door. Sandra slammed the door shut and was all over her brothers.

"Are y'all fuckin' crazy? I know that grimy bitch. Her stage name is Chocolate. She's a cold freak."

"Why you dissin' my joint like that, Sandra?" Rishon asked moving closer to his sister.

"Rishon, you fool. I hope you really not serious about that ho? Please, don't get my brothers in no beef over that bitch."

Rishon raised his hand to hit Sandra, but Cornelius grabbed him just in time.

"Chill little brother. You can hit your chick if you want, but not my little sister. Go ahead, Sandy. Keep talking."

"Big bro, that scandalous bitch used to work with me at the Goat in Hunts Point. She fucks hard for that paper. She's also a dyke. I freaked off with her one night myself. Trust me when I tell y'all brothers, she ain't worth none of this drama."

They all stared at Rishon. Realizing that all eyes were on him, Rishon said, "Hold up. If what Sandra said is true, because we all know she be lying her ass off, but if it's true, all chicks got their past and skeletons. Look at you, Sandra. You're a crack-head lesbian, who are you to judge? But the fact is, I love Elaine and she loves me. So she's staying. Yo, this ain't even about Elaine no more. These niggas rollin' up in our hood on some gangster shit. Where that gonna leave us? Dead and stinkin'? We got to defend ours. That's what this is about," Rishon said, trying to take the sting out of what Sandra told his brothers.

"After hearing about that chick you still want her for your girl, little brother? You buggin', but that's on you. One thing for certain and two things for sure we ain't gonna let no outta area niggas roll up in our hood and not defend it, that ain't happening," Cornelius said, checking the artillery.

"Rishon, you always getting into some shit, now you got us all involved. We all got beef with Malik from back in the days, but this shit really started over a piece of ass. And that ain't cool, little brother," Heckie said before joining Cornelius at the gun table.

"Now that we got Sandra's bullshit out the way, we can get back to the business at hand."

"Over a bitch, that's crazy y'all," Sandra said. Turning to Rishon, she continued. "Baby brother, I hope you don't live to regret this shit you about to cause. A lot of people will probably get hurt and for what, a dick sucking, pussy eating, freak that goes to the highest bidder? Rishon, you always were a sucker for the bitches."

Sandra walked to where Heckie and Cornelius were sitting and gave them kisses on their cheeks.

"Be careful," she said, walking out of the apartment.

Rishon locked the door, and walked back over to his brothers.

"Good-looking out on keeping it real with me, I won't ever forget this," said a humble Rishon.

"Whatever man, let's just get everything ready," Heckie said, loading a fresh clip into an AK-47.

Chapter 04

Hell was coming from Harlem in the form of a convoy of SUV's. They pulled into a parking lot of a shopping plaza's on White Plains Road after exiting the Bruckner Expressway. The vehicles emptied, his boys and their mercenaries all gathered around Malik's car to receive their final instructions.

"Listen up so y'all can know what's going on. We're gonna surround the Commons and at exactly one a.m. Everyone will bum-rush the front, back and side entrances at the same time. Now remember whoever finds Elaine first, bring her directly to me. And she better not be hurt," ordered Malik. .

"Check your burners and make sure you got enough shots," added Hill.

When everybody was certain of their assignments, positions

and all the weapons were checked the men all piled back into the trucks and headed down White Plains Road toward Stevenson Commons. Nearing Seward Avenue, the convoy parked down a side street. Like any army on maneuvers, the men piled out the trucks and set up a perimeter around the Commons in two minutes. Malik looked on from his makeshift headquarters in the park across the street, and he was impressed.

"AG, you sure trained these cats in the short time you had. I just hope they do as well when we rush these fools."

Everyone was in position waiting for the final word. The streets appeared deadly silent.

"Okay Hill, let's get ready to rock and roll," said Malik.

Hill, a few of his men, and Malik started to cross Seward Avenue. The lookouts saw Malik advancing. They signaled other lookouts posted up around the buildings. With the assault in progress, everyone started to rush to their assigned entrances.

Pop, pop, pop—out of nowhere shots were fired. Bullets rained from the rooftops and the apartments facing the street. Malik and his men were totally taken by surprise. Three of the men were hit.

"Oh bum-rush the fuckin' spot, huh…? Be in and out before they know we're there. Yo Malik, how the fuck they know we coming? They were just laying on us. We could have all been murdered," shouted a furious Big-O at his boy.

"How the hell do I know?" asked Malik, looking around at

the men in the park. "I guess niggas just talk too fucking much! You know how it is when two people know sump'n. It'll never be a secret again. Hill, A.G., Big-O, Nes, let's build."

The five men walked over to the other side of the park to re-group, and plan their next strategy.

"Okay it's obvious. These Bronx shooters can't hit shit. Only a few soldiers got hit, and they had us dead to right. Listen, we got some infra-red scoped rifles. Let's set up a few men behind some cars and pick off a few of their snipers. We can lessen the odds a bit," said AG.

"Do y'all hear this? This cat reads the art of war, now he's Hannibal and shit," said Malik, laughing and the rest of the crew joined in.

"No playa, we just buggin'. That's a good idea. It does lessen the odds, for real," Nes said.

"Okay, you know your boys better than I do. Whoever you know that can shoot good, set them up with the rifles, and let them get busy," ordered Malik.

The next several minutes brought sniper fire. There were exchanges between both sides. The plan worked as AG had hoped. His boys did take out a few of the opposition, but he lost a few men in the process.

"This ain't getting us anywhere. We've been here for an hour and we're no closer to the inside of the Commons than when we got here. Yo Big-O, get off the phone. This shit is serious," said Malik.

"So is this call, Malik. I think I found a way that we can find out what we are really up against, and how organized their crew really is," said Big-O.

"What you talking about, O?" Hill asked with a puzzled look on his grill.

"I called my peeps from Castle Hill. She'll be here in a few minutes. Then I'll tell you what's up."

The men waited in the park, a taxi pulled up to the curb and a pregnant girl wobbled out of the back seat.

"Hey, Big-O, did I take too long? Well, I'm ready when you are," said the pregnant girl, entering the park.

"Sharon, these are my boys. No time for introductions. You know what I need you to do right?" asked Big-O.

"Yeah Big-O, I got you. But you sure I won't be in any danger?"

"C'mon girl, I'd rather stick my hand in a fan than put you or my nephew in harm's way. Just go do your stuff. You always braggin' about all those acting classes you took. Hell, since I paid for them, start acting."

"Okay Big-O, I'm out. Watch and learn."

Sharon wobbled across the street in a real exaggerated walk. She was even groaning.

"What the hell is she doing and what's this all about, O?" inquired Malik looking annoyed.

"We need to find out how strong they are right? So my girl is gonna get that info for us, just chill and watch," said Big-O.

The men watched the pregnant woman approaching the barricaded front entrance. Her groan grew even louder. When she was directly in front of the entrance she took out a bottle of water and secretly poured it down the front of her dress before falling to the ground.

"Oh God help, somebody…! My water broke. I think I'm going to have my baby now! Please somebody help me! Don't let my baby die in the street. Please God help me!"

There were no signs of response from anyone in the building. Her wailing continued and she saw movement coming from the front lobby. It seemed like some men at the front entrance were trying to decide what to do.

"Oh God, I feel the baby's head coming!"

The barricade was removed and three heavily armed men came out. They surrounded the woman. Two men and a woman picked her up and helped Sharon inside the building. The three armed men ran back, putting up the barricade.

"Big-O, you are a fuckin' genius. Damn y'all need to be in the marines or some shit. Y'all got the ill tactics," exclaimed Malik, feeling optimistic.

The men waited in the park and snipers continued their periodic shootouts. About a half an hour went by then suddenly the barricades came down and again the front door opened. Coming out of the front door was the pregnant girl and she was going bananas.

"What kind of busted building is this? You have no electricity and you can't even call for an ambulance. Let me out of this asylum. I'll walk to the damn hospital."

Going in, she knew that they couldn't call an ambulance. Big-O told her that one of their men was an expert computer hacker. He used his computers to shut down the power all over the Stevenson Commons complex. He even cut the power in a ten-block radius so the police wouldn't be notified. His special device even blocked out cell phone transmissions in the area except for their own phones. Eventually the siege would be exposed so they had to move fast.

Sharon came wobbling across the street and went to Big-O. She told him what she saw inside the buildings then wobbled up the street to catch a cab back home.

"I got some good news, and some bad news. My girl said they don't have a strong crew, but the place is pretty well locked down. They got couches, chairs and even cars blocking the entrances, plus men on each side of every roof."

"Okay, what's the good news?" asked Hill.

"She said they got an underground garage and the stairs down there leads right up into the courtyard. And the garage isn't barricaded," added Big-O.

"Bet that's how we can get in. Let's do this, yo," said Malik, grinning.

"I don't know, Hill. This shit looks too easy," Nes said to his boy.

The two of them and four of their boys approached the stairs in the underground garage. "I ain't feeling this, man. Send some men in the stairwell to see if everything's okay."

Hill thought about it for a second then sent the men in. The men entered the stairs and checked the steps before cautiously climbing them. Hill and Nes stood by the door waiting. They heard a barrage of gunshots and then the men crying out in agony. Hill and Nes ran to the stairs and started to go inside, but shots went whizzing over their heads.

"No wonder it wasn't barricaded—it was a fucking trap. Big-O, you sure that chick wasn't setting us up?" asked Malik with a suspicious look on his mug.

"Man that's family. I know she ain't crossing me."

The men looked at each other in silence. They all had the same thoughts. AG finally walked over to Malik and asked, "Is she worth all this man?"

Chapter 05

The Stevenson Commons siege was going on for about two hours already, and neither side was getting the advantage. The only real casualties were from the sniper fire from both sides. Rishon and his boys inside the Commons did not dare venture out into the open and Malik's forces were unable to infiltrate the barricaded buildings. Things remained at a standstill until the arrival of Rishon's cousin.

"Open up the back gate barricade. That's my cousin. It's about fucking time he got here."

Rishon had been walking in the courtyard stressing, over his next move when his cousin arrived. The enemy soldiers had the buildings surrounded, Rishon cousin, Rob came around to the back entrance. There were only two lookouts. Malik's men saw Rob's crew approach, and ran to inform him.

"Yo Malik, about ten men just pulled up to the rear exit gate and went inside. They were strapped heavy. I guess your boy, Rishon, went and got himself some back up. What we gon' do now, my brother?"

"Don't sweat it. Them cats are just gonna be locked up in the building like the rest of them coward ass cats. Let's just wait and see their next move while we plan ours. Go back and hold down your spot."

"Rishon wouldn't just have them come over here unless he was planning on using them. So let's be extra careful," added Big-O.

"Damn it took you long enough, Rob. But I'm glad you came to hold a brother down. Good looking out," Rishon said to his cousin Rob.

"Yeah well, I'm here. So let's get busy," said Rob, smirking.

"What do you suggest, Rob? You got a plan?" asked Cornelius.

"I noticed that the only place that Malik's crew is strong is out front on Lafayette Avenue. The back and side gates are being watched by only a few of his men."

"What you saying, Rob?" asked a clueless Rishon.

"Try and keep up man. I'm gonna take a few of my boys and bag up a couple of his boys. You feel me?"

"No question. Let's make that happen," said Rishon.

Rob and his heavily armed men did just that. They started

at the east gate and snuck out to ambush the unsuspecting lookouts. After they took them totally by surprise, they tied them up, and brought them inside to the complex. This was repeated at two more locations. The battle would have taken a worse turn for Malik's forces, but he got lucky.

"Rishon, I just got finished talking with Heckie. He tells me this beef is really about you and some stripper broad. Nigga, I know you ain't get me down here to fuckin' risk me and my boys' lives over a bitch?" asked Rob.

"No big cuz. She ain't just some chick. She's going to be my wife. I love her. Plus this is about Malik trying to rush our hood.

"Your hood, playa…? You're family and all and that's why I came. But my men ain't risking their lives over no damn chick and I ain't either. Sorry cuz, but we did our share. Peace!"

Rob and his crew left out of the back gate, and went back to their own hood. Standing in the courtyard with Rishon, were Heckie and Cornelius. They joined him shortly after Rob had left.

"Heckie, why you tell Rob this beef was over Elaine?"

"A man has the right to know why he's risking his life. I guess he didn't appreciate that too much, huh?" said Heckie, smiling.

"Hill, the cats that came a while ago just broke out. It don't look like they coming back," informed one of Hill's crew.

Hill went over to where Malik and his boys were sitting on a park bench.

"My boy just told me that Rishon's reinforcements just broke out."

"Word…? That might be a break for us. Let's just hope it's not another trap," said Nes.

The men were contemplating what Hill just told them, AG then took a picture out of his pocket and looked at it lustfully.

"When this shit's over, the first thing that I'm doing is hitting this little shorty I met last week at a club," said AG, handing the photo to Malik.

"Damn she's thick, but she looks crazy familiar, don't she Nes?"

Nes glanced at the photo, and a shocked look appeared on his face. He looked at Hill. Hill seeing the expression on his face instantly looked at the photo before Nes could hide it. Looking at the half-naked picture Hill shouted, "What the fuck you doing with my baby mom's picture?"

The park got deadly silent for a second then AG said. "Oh shit, Hill, that's my word. I didn't know that was your baby moms. Man, you know I never would have hit…"

Realizing his poor choice of words, AG stopped talking.

"You fucked her? Oh shit! You dirty muthafucka!"

Hill tried to rush AG, but Nes and Big-O grabbed him.

"Chill baby boy, how could he know that was your baby

mother? Listen it's fucked up but this ain't the time to deal with this. Let's not forget where we are and why we're here," said Nes.

"This nigga fucked my girl," said Hill, walking away.

Patrick came running over. "Hill, where you going?"

Hill turned to his friend and then looked at the rest of the men.

"I can't stay here with this piece of shit. I'm out y'all. I can't believe this shit, my own boy."

Hill then left the park and went to his truck, and drove off, leaving his boys to their fate.

"That's just fucking great! We done lost one of our best troopers over a bitch," yelled Malik to his remaining crew.

"Yeah well, we're here because of a..." Big-O stopped short, not wanting to disrespect Malik.

"Hill and his crew left, we have been getting dogged. His snipers were holding us down nicely. Now it seems like we're just sitting out here holding our dicks. Anyone got any suggestions?" asked Malik.

"We could try and rush one of the other gates and see if we can get inside and end this. The firing from across the street is bullshit, plus we ain't got a lot more time. It's just a matter of time before police roll by, and then it's a wrap," warned Nes, cleaning his Glock.

"Shit, right about now, I'll try anything. Take some men and try that back door. See if we get lucky."

Nes took five men and snuck around to the back where Rob and his crew exited. Using several long iron pipes, the men attempted to pry the gated fence open. The gate began to break loose from the concrete wall and they heard men rushing toward them from the other side.

"Fall back… Hurry…!"

Nes and his men backed away from the gate. Several shots from a machine gun hit the metal gate followed by raucous laughter.

"They think a nigga ain't ready they buggin'. This is my hood! Y'all never getting up in here," said Rishon to Elaine while looking out an apartment window facing the park where Malik set up his base camp.

"Rishon, I'm tired of all this shooting, and for what? I ain't going back to Malik anyway, so he might as well just break out," said Elaine, walking over to the window.

"That pussy of yours will make niggas do crazy shit, baby. You can see that. He can't stay out there forever. Po-po will get wind of this real soon, trust me."

Elaine bent over to look out the window. Rishon noticed that she wasn't wearing any panties under her short skirt. Taking out his penis, he walked up behind her. Rishon lifted up Elaine's dress. She turned and smiled when she saw his erection. Rishon slid into her moist and snapping turtle pussy, moaning, "Shit, any nigga would go to war over this pussy."

Chapter 06

"I can't believe the police haven't come by yet. Just because the power is off and the cell phones don't work, all that is doing is buying us some time. Our luck can't stay like this," Nes said.

"Yeah, I know Nes. I think we got until dawn before the spot gets blown up, so stop being so scary. It's just a matter of time before we get into the Commons or those cats slip up. We got this I know it," said Malik, not only trying to reassure Nes, but the other discouraged soldiers in the park.

"We lost a few more men just now and we're still at square one. For real, the men are ready to break out. Money or no money, they're not trying to sit and wait for police. Malik, either we make a power move soon or it's a wrap," argued AG.

Big-O nodded his head in agreement while Malik stood

silent for a while. There was a possibility that he could indeed lose his discouraged recruits. He turned to his boys.

"Listen, we know why we're here. This all my beef, and believe me, I respect the fact that y'all rolled with me on the strength. I know everybody is fed up and stressed, but just give me a little longer. If we still don't have Elaine in a few, all of you can break out. As far as I'm concerned, you would've kept your word as brothers, cool."

Malik's boys looked at each other then turned to Malik and said, "Cool."

Rishon and his brothers were in his apartment, talking about their defenses and the possibility of an offense when the apartment door swung open and Sandra stormed into the room.

"Look even cousin Rob broke out. You got to send that chick packing before something bad happens."

Cornelius looked at her puzzled and asked, "What you talking about, sis?"

"What I mean is, I have a funny feeling about this, and you know my dreams always come true. Well, I dreamt that those guys outside, got inside and a lot of people were hurt and killed. Please y'all, fuck what Rishon think he's feeling for that ho. She's bad news. Cancel that bitch!"

Hearing his baby sister's plea, Heckie turned to Rishon and

said, "What do you think about all this? We lost some good men tonight. And we're captives in our own building and that's because of your chick. Don't you think it's time you sent her home?"

"She is home. This is her home now. She's gonna be wifey. If y'all don't wanna help me defend mines any longer, that's cool. But Elaine stays," shouted Rishon, storming out of the apartment like he was drunk on love.

Sandra was right behind Rishon on her way to the other apartment where Elaine was staying to have it out with her. She passed an apartment, and heard loud moaning coming from inside. The door was slightly ajar and Sandra slowed down. Being nosey, Sandra just had to look inside. When she opened the door, she shook her head and smiled. Two apartment doors away from Rishon's, and his girl Elaine was bent over a couch in a living room, giving it up to two of his boys.

Elaine was giving one man a blow job while the other was hittin her from behind. Sandra watched the freak show, and started getting horny. She started rubbing her hand against her pussy. Elaine was going off on the two young men while Sandra's fingers started going wild inside her moist cavity.

"Sandra, what the fuck are you doing?"

Sandra spun around to see her brother Heckie looking at her in disgust.

"Heckie, I... I..."

Feeling embarrassed Sandra suddenly shifted the attention

from herself. "Shush Heckie, come here and check this bitch out."

Heckie hesitated at first still angry at his sister's sexual display. He was about to walk away and heard moans coming from the apartment. Recognizing that voice when she screamed, "Fuck me harder! Ah yes, c'mon harder…!"

Heckie almost wished he didn't recognize the voice, but he did. He walked over to the door and pushed it open.

"Oh shit, Heckie! Damn!" said one of the men, turning around.

"You niggas are crazy. That shit is real grimy. Get the fuck out!"

The two men looked at each other and grabbed their clothes running out the apartment. They didn't even glance at Elaine. Sandra stood by the door waiting for Heckie to go off on Elaine. She saw Elaine go to work.

"Heckie, I'm so sorry and ashamed. I don't know what got over me. This drama has Rishon so distant from me. I just…" said a butt naked, Elaine.

She seductively started walking toward Heckie. Seeing his erection she walked over to the door and said before closing it, "Heckie, please let me explain."

"What's up, Big-O? You've been kinda silent for a while now.

What's on your mind?" AG asked.

"AG, this shit can't continue. We need an edge to get this shit over with and soon. I'm gonna go check Hill and see if he will stop acting like a bitch and come back to the set. But check it, even if he doesn't, I've been thinking about something. I'm not sure of all the details yet, but when I get it figured out my plan just might put an end to this bullshit, for real."

Chapter 07

"Hill, you know you on some real bullshit, kid. We been boys since the seventies and you just gonna leave us uptown in the middle of beef over a chick?"

Big O seeing hill didn't like the chick comment changed his tone. He had driven back to Harlem and found Hill in the Lenox Lounge. Big-O didn't want to be too hard on him. He found him at a corner of the bar, nursing his pride with a bottle.

"I know she's your baby mother but the two of you are separated. She moved on. C'mon, I doubt if either of them knew the history the other one had with you. Listen man, forget about this bullshit and keep it moving."

"I hear you, O. It's just that every time I picture his dick up in my puss... Or my ex-pussy for that matter, I get mad tight. I know AG… None of you would push up on one of my chicks past or present, if y'all knew she belonged to me." Hill looked at Big-O. "How's the beef going anyway?"

"Time's running out. We only have a few hours before the police roll around. Malik and the rest of us have decided to holla at bitch-ass Rishon. See if him and his boys wanna go head-up in the little courtyard outside the Commons. That area will be like neutral ground, get this shit over with, last man standing type a shit," said Big-O.

"That's some real *West Side Story* shit, but it will definitely settle the war."

"You gonna be there or what? We need you for real. This won't start until I get back with or without you. Everyone is hoping it's with you," said Big-O and took a swig of Hennessey.

Big-O sat next to his friend and shared a drink. Hill sipped, reflected for a minute and a smile creased the sides of his mouth.

"I remember I was on the block flossing one night, and these niggas from Brooklyn tried to stick me up for my sheepskin. AG saw them from his window, he ran downstairs with his old-ass 22, busting at them kids. He was always there for me, man. Yeah, I'll be there in a few.

"A'ight Hill, we'll be waiting. Hurry," Big-O said, leaving the lounge, smiling. He jumped into his whip and headed back to the Bronx.

"So what you gonna do, Rishon? It's your call, man. These cats want to have an all-out man-to-man war. I already picked out who we would roll with. I just need to know if you down. This your beef," Heckie sarcastically said to Rishon.

He heard the proposal Malik had one of his men delivered. Rishon looked at Elaine. She had her eyes on Heckie. Rishon finally made a decision.

"Hell, I'm down. We'll meet them faggots out front. Make sure we got some cats by the entrance, you know just in case they're trying to play us."

Cornelius walked to the front entrance. Malik's messenger was waiting for an answer.

"Yo, we agree to that playa. We'll roll with ten men and you bring your ten and let's get busy.

The messenger ran back to Malik's camp and informed them of the response.

"Where's Big-O? They gonna be coming out any minute now."

Malik's crew was making the final preparations for the fight.

Big-O's car was spotted turning the corner. When Big-O walked in the park without Hill the vibes suddenly changed.

"I guess our boy for twenty years is going to front on us," said AG in anger.

"Nah AG, chill with that, man. Hill's on his way. Then it'll be on," said Big-O.

The barricade to the front entrance came down and Cornelius, Heckie and Rishon came out and stood in front of the building.

"Oh shit, they ready man. How we gonna stall them until Hill gets here?" asked a surprised Nes.

"We're not. If we start hesitating, they gonna think we pussy and just go back inside. All this shit would just be for nothing. No we gonna go without Hill. We got nine cats already, just pick one more trooper and let's rush these fools," said Malik with a deadly grin on his mug.

His longing for his bride had left him desperate. Now he was reacting out of pure love.

"Who the hell we gonna pick that can replace bad-ass Hill. C'mon already, man...!"

"I'll go..."

The men turned to see Patrick, Hill's friend standing there trying his best to look hard.

"Nigga please, this ain't no baking contest. This real beef... Now stop playing," laughed AG.

"No, hold up. Hill told me dude got black belts for all types of shit. He's nice with his hands, man. Y'all know Hill ain't gonna front about no shit like that. Patrick, you really know all that martial arts shit, man?"

Patrick walked over to the park bench and closed his eyes. Letting out a loud yell, he raised his hand over his head then brought it down on the back of the bench, splitting the wood.

"Oh shit! That was ill. Let's bring this cat for real," yelled an excited Malik.

Even though there were men all around him, Rishon's voice sounded nervous, shouting from across the street. Malik and his men turned to hear him talking shit.

"What y'all punk-ass-niggas waiting for...? We here now, let's do this," said Rishon.

Malik and his crew stepped to them. All hell broke loose. Malik had a deadly look on his face when his eyes saw the smile on Rishon's face.

"Come get some of this, niggas! Yeah, I'm fucking your wife!"

Malik bugged out, and fearlessly rushed Rishon. The other men separated engaging adversaries. Heckie jumped on Big-O. Cornelius grappled with AG while Nes was already beating down two other men. The battle raged on, knives were drawn, combatants ending up being sliced on their hands, chest, and faces.

It was agreed that no guns would be brought to the

courtyard. This war appeared to be about one crew defending their turf against a takeover. The real cause was a scandalous, stripper named Elaine.

"Fuck! Look at that bridge!"

Hill reached 125th and saw that the bridge to the Bronx was jam packed. He sat in traffic honking his horn while cursing loudly. Hill had a strong notion that something bad was about to happen.

"I should be there with my friends..." mumbled Hill, pulling out a blunt.

The pre-dawn battle was in full swing. Several of the combating soldiers were badly injured and left the fighting to tend to their wounds. Ten men were left fighting in the front courtyard. Malik and Rishon had discarded their weapons. They fought fist to fist. It was more personal that way. AG had been stabbed in the leg, but he kept fighting. Cornelius and Heckie were holding their own. Big-O had knocked out several of the opposition.

The fighting casualties were fairly equal. Both sides lost the same amount of men. Patrick surprised everybody by fighting like a true warrior. He had beat down many men with his martial arts fighting style. He was punishing one of Rishon's men, when someone spun him around and punched him in the face.

Patrick saw Heckie standing in front of him. Heckie used to be a semi-pro wrestler before he started dealing drugs. The two men circled, feeling out each other. Patrick threw a kick that caught Heckie flush in the grill. Heckie quickly shrugged it off, and was caught with another and another. Patrick was way too fast for Heckie's defenses. Heckie couldn't get close enough to attack the martial arts expert.

Patrick threw so many kicks he suddenly became very tired. Heckie saw this and took advantage. The last kick that Patrick threw was very slow and weak. Heckie timed it perfectly, and grabbed Patrick's extended leg, while coming up under him and scooped him off the ground. Heckie lifted the frail Patrick over his shoulders and body-slammed him on the concrete.

The bone shattering noise could be heard throughout the fighting ranks. All of the combatants stopped fighting and looked at the limp, broken body of Patrick. Malik, AG, Nes, and Big-O ran over to the body. They all shook their heads in sorrow.

Chapter 08

The death of Patrick caused both sides to declare a truce. They would use the time to tend to the wounded and take Patrick's body off the street. They brought their fallen soldier inside the park. Rishon had a deep stab wound on his right arm. He went to Elaine, seeking first-aid for his injury.

"Baby, I got cut. Go get the first aid kit out the bathroom cabinet, and help me sterilize the wound."

Sandra was there silently watching her brother. She decided not to tell Rishon what she had seen Elaine doing. She wanted him to see how grimy his lover was for himself. He probably wouldn't believe her anyway.

Rishon walked over to the couch where Elaine was watching television he noticed she didn't even look in his direction.

"Oh baby, I'm sorry you're hurt, but I just did my nails and they're wet. Can you ask somebody else to help you with your little cut? Thanks baby," said Elaine, without glancing at Rishon's bloody arm.

Rishon stared at her in complete shock and wondering. How could a woman he loved so much and claimed loved him, be so cold and unfeeling? He thought silently to himself then Rishon remembered all that his sister had told him. He started having doubts. Without saying a word to Elaine, Rishon walked out of the apartment with the first aid kit under his arm.

A makeshift headquarters in the park was a place of silent mourning. Patrick was not the only casualty of the skirmish, but he volunteered to fight and lost his life, that made everyone feel the loss even more.

The men talked about the events and everyone had mixed feelings about their purpose for being there. They all agreed on one thing—it was time to go.

Everyone was conversing when Hill's truck pulled up to the curb in front of the park. Hill walked into the park and immediately sensed something was wrong.

"Sorry I'm late y'all. There was mad traffic coming across the bridge."

"You're more than a little late cat, it's over," said Malik with anger in his voice.

Hill ignored Malik's comment and walked over to AG.

"I'm sorry I'm late. We have to talk later okay?"

AG hugged his lifelong friend for a few seconds. Hill and AG parted then Hill went to talk briefly to Nes and Big-O before he looked around and made the dreaded inquiry.

"Yo, where's Patrick? I know he didn't break out after I left. That's just not his style."

The mention of Patrick's name brought a solemn reaction. Hill's face turned pale and he started walking around the park calling out Patrick's name over and over. Big-O caught up to him.

"Hill, I got to talk to you. Some fucked up shit happened. It's about Patrick."

Looking at Big-O's expression Hill knew it was bad news. Hill turned and continued to call out his friend's name. "Yo Pat, Pat where are you, man?"

"Damn my brother, I'm sorry but Pats dead," said Big-O.

Hill stopped dead in his tracks and spun around to face Big-O. Through his peripheral vision, he caught sight of a lifeless body lying on a bench. He walked over closer to the bench and his knees buckled when he saw the ashy-gray face of his expressionless friend.

Kneeling down and tenderly caressing Patrick's face, Hill openly cried. Most of the men looked at him, feeling his pain. The way Hill held Patrick confirmed what was suspected about their relationship. They were more than friends, but nobody commented on the heartfelt moment.

The scene between the two men lasted about fifteen minutes then suddenly rage appeared on Hill's face and he stood up.

"Who did this?"

Wiping the tears from his eyes, Hill walked over to Nes and Big-O. "Who did this?" he demanded.

Nes looked at AG and then at Hill before saying, "It was Heckie, but, yo, I don't think he meant to kill him, man." Nes paused for a beat before continuing. "We were fighting hand-to-hand so we could settle this. And shit just got out of hand. I'm sorry, partner."

Immediately Hill started across the street. He got to the other side and stood by the entrance to the Commons.

"Heckie, Heckie, yo, you killed my boy. Muthafucka, now I'm a kill you. This beef ends now with me and you, just the two of us, nigga. Hand to hand homey until one of us stops breathing. Let's see you kill me. You a bad-ass nigga, right Heckie?"

There was no response from the building for a few minutes. Hill shouted a variety of insults at Heckie and the barricade came down. Seconds after the gates were flung open Heckie walked out into the courtyard to face Hill.

"Listen, I didn't mean to kill your boy. He just fell wrong and his neck broke. It really wasn't my intention, it really was an accident."

Hill didn't hear what Heckie saying. All he saw was the one who had murdered his friend. Hill rushed Heckie and caught him with a right cross in the jaw. Heckie was big and stout but the power of Hill's punch knocked him to the ground.

He was all over Heckie, punching him in the face repeatedly and crying at the same time. Heckie knew that he had to get up off the floor. Heckie swung his right leg under Hill's legs and swept him off his feet. He was now able to stand up. Heckie knew there was no reasoning with Hill and he had to fight fiercely to survive.

The two men started boxing. This was Hill's specialty. Hill threw several quick jabs to Heckie's face and drew first blood. His one-two combination from the stomach to the temple sent Heckie flying several feet across the courtyard. Heckie was out-matched and laid on the floor fearing for his life. Dazed from the volley of punches, he reached into his Timberland boots and pulled out a long sharp throwing knife.

Hill saw the blade and reached down pulling out his own. Suddenly Heckie jumped to his feet, and got off the first throw. Had Heckie not have been dazed by Hill's intense punches his weapon might have found its mark. Hill's reflexes however were sharpened by his anger, and he ducked the razor sharp projectile. Sidestepping the weapon, he released his own. The knife found its target.

Gasping for breath Heckie put his hand around the blade that protruded from his throat. Blood poured freely from the wound, and Heckie's eyes took on a lifeless appearance.

"That was for my friend," said Hill, walking over and yanking the knife out of the wound.

More blood gushed from Heckie's neck. He looked at Hill, not seeing or hearing him. Heckie crumbled to the pavement dying before reaching it.

Hill picked up Heckie's body and flung it over his shoulders. The men in the park stared at Hill puzzled, while the people in the building looked on helplessly. In minutes tires were heard screeching around the corner. Anyone who had witnessed this sight must have thought that Hill had gone mad. He drove down Lafayette Avenue circling Stevenson Commons, dragging the lifeless body of Heckie behind his truck.

Malik and the men looked on in horror as Hill drove around the entire Commons several times, screaming out of his window. The death of Patrick had driven Hill mad with vengeance and the men on both sides were furious with his disrespect toward the body.

When Nes could take it no longer he took out his Glock and walked into the street. Hill's truck came around the corner and Nes opened fire. The automatic spat and three of the truck's tires were blown, causing it to swerve, before slowly hitting the curb.

"What the fuck you doing, Nes…?" shouted Hill, coming out the truck screaming mad.

"You buggin', Hill. That shit you did was some caveman bullshit. You were violating that man's body. That shit was foul. It's over."

Nes walked to the back of Hill's truck and took out his knife cutting the rope that tied Heckie's torn and broken body to the truck. Nes lifted up the body and flung it over his shoulders. Walking to the front of the building, he laid Heckie on the bench, and left.

"I'm sorry, ma. I didn't mean for Heckie to get… Ah killed. It's… Really all my fault," said Rishon, sounding emotional.

His parents had helplessly watching the horror show going on in the streets with Hill and Heckie's body. His mother looked at Rishon with hate written on her face. They watched Nes carrying Heckie's body over his shoulders. Rishon ordered two men to get his brother's body.

"Don't touch my son!" yelled Heckie's mother. "I will go take care of my baby." Heckie's mother along with his somber father went to get their son's battered body. Together they brought it inside.

"We gotta be out of here, man. What Hill did was crazy wrong," said AG, getting his boys ready to leave.

"AG, you and your cats, hold up. Let's not forget why we're here. Elaine is still inside and we got about two hours before daylight. I ain't leavin' without her," said Malik with conviction.

"Malik, I think we did our best, man. Sometimes you have to cut your losses and hang it up. I think now is one of those times," said Nes, agreeing with AG.

Malik saw Hill's at his truck, changing his flat tires. He called out to Hill, "Yo Hill, I need to talk to you." He turned to his boys and said, "Let's see what Hill says about leaving."

Hill had a deranged look on his face when he stood up to

walk over to the park. He reached the middle of the street, and shots rang out. The first bullet entered Hill's foot below the right ankle. The second one went through his back and entered his heart killing him instantly. The men in the park started shooting back at the building. A few went and dragged Hill's body from the middle of the street.

"You cats still wanna leave,? They just broke the truce and murdered Hill right in front of us," said Malik, looking at Hill's body.

"Malik, Hill was my boy too. But that shit he did to Heckie's body was a violation. I ain't no big religious brother but that might just have been God's justice. Let's just bounce," said AG with tears in his eyes.

"Let's just get the fuck out of here," said Nes. His tone was very emotional.

"I told all of you cats, I ain't leaving," shouted Malik.

"I think I can put a stop to this, once and for all," said Big-O.

Everyone looked at Big-O and gathered around to hear what he had to say.

"I'm feeling that. I think that shit can work. I'm down with that plan. What about you cats?" asked Malik.

"I don't know, man…" said AG.

"I'm with AG on that, I don't know if that shit will work either," said Nes, sounding skeptical.

"I know that Hill violated, and maybe that was the price he had to pay. I don't know. But it doesn't change the fact that they broke the truce and killed our boy. I just can't let that go. No disrespect, Malik. But fuck Elaine at this point. I'm going in for my own reasons" said Big-O.

"Y'all cats with this, or not?" asked Malik, looking at Big-O, but not commenting.

He knew he needed as many allies as possible to pull the caper off. There was contemplative silence. The men took a turn and examined the situation. Then Nes looked at AG and they both looked at Hill's body.

"Let's get this over with, man," said Nes.

"What you mean they just left like that?" asked Sandra.

Cornelius and Rishon were standing in front of Stevenson Commons. They had gone outside because lookouts reported Malik and his entire crew left the park, driving in the direction of the highway. Rishon and a few of his men followed by Sandra and Cornelius came outside to check on the report.

"Them cowards really left. They knew what time it was. They had no wins with the kid," boasted Rishon.

"Rishon, they left this fly-ass Navigator by the park. I think it belonged to Hill. It has two flat tires," reported one of Rishon's boys, after checking the park across the street.

"Word, that shit was Hill's. It's mine now. He won't need it where he's at. A few of y'all push that shit around the back. Leave it in the underground garage. I'll hook it up tomorrow," smiled a confident Rishon.

"This shit just looks too easy to me. I don't think this shit is over, Cornelius," whispered Sandra to her brother.

She shook her head and walked back inside, looking at the men pushing the vehicle across the street.

Chapter 09

Malik and his men had left the park and it seemed abandoned the siege on Stevenson Commons. The entire population of the building started to celebrate. Rishon had this moment planned. He had his men bring up all the food and stashed cases of Hennessey and Moet champagne. They broke out the exotic weed and everybody got tore-down, having fun.

Rishon took on an aura of invincibility. The victory over Malik along with the effect of the liquor and weed had Rishon acting like he singlehandedly saved the Commons.

When the sun started to peak out over the horizon it found the occupants of Stevenson Commons all stuck on high and drunk. Some residents staggered back to their apartments, while others crashed out, sleeping in the courtyard on the benches and in the grass. Sandra was still having doubts and didn't celebrate. Instead she went straight to bed, but not before warning Rishon and his men to watch their backs.

"You hear that, AG?" asked Malik from a hidden compartment under Hill's truck.

Hill used to make drug runs down south in his truck and he built a hidden compartment behind the back seat. It wasn't very big but if situated just right, it could easily hold two grown men.

"Hear what, man? I don't hear shit," replied AG, getting very uncomfortable in the stash compartment.

"That's just it. It's dead silent, cat. I think we can get out now."

AG and Malik opened up the hidden compartment and cautiously came out, looking around. The garage was dark and packed with cars in every parking spot. The only light visible was from the emergency lights in the stairwell leading up to the inner courtyard.

"AG, let's see what's up, and remember stick to the plan."

The two men walked to the staircase and started climbing the stairs. When they got to the top they put their ears to the door, but still only silence.

"Here we go, homey," said AG, pushing the door open and

peeking inside.

Scattered around the courtyard were a few men and women knocked out sleeping and snoring, dead to the world. Doubting that everyone in the complex was asleep, they moved quickly before being seen.

Malik walked cautiously but quickly to the front entrance and quietly removed the barricades and opened the gates. Big-O, Nes and a few of their mercenaries were waiting on the other side to get in. Malik smile when saw them.

"Hurry up. You cats know what to do," ordered Malik as the men entered the Commons.

The men scattered around the building. A few of them were carrying buckets of gasoline. They started pouring the gas on every floor of the complex. The men gathered in the courtyard after the entire place was soaked with gas.

"Listen, when we light these fires, all hell will break loose. Cats will be running around in crazy panic. There's going to be shooting. Please don't shoot each other or me in the chaos. Whoever finds Elaine come get me right away, and that bitch-ass, Rishon too."

The orders were given and the men set fire to the buildings. Couple seconds were all it took for the people of Stevenson Commons to smell smoke. They quickly realize what had happened.

"Fire, fire…! Oh shit the whole place is burning," said a pregnant woman, running out of her apartment.

Men came running out in their boxers and briefs. They saw

their opposition and knew they were in grave danger. Malik and his men started shooting at the fleeing occupants of the building. They tried not to hit any women or children but with the smoke and confusion many innocent people were injured.

The few of Rishon's men who actually came out armed were instantly and mercilessly gunned down. Malik walked around the courtyard amongst the chaos, and heard someone calling his name from one of the apartment windows.

"Malik, we found your girl and Rishon. Homeboy was hiding under the bed. Man, come on up to 412."

Malik and Nes walked up the stairs to the fourth floor. They found the door.

"In here," said the man who called out to Malik.

He was standing in the doorway as they approached the apartment. Nes walked in the door followed by Malik. When they entered, Rishon and Elaine were sitting on the couch. Big-O held a pistol pointing directly at Rishon's head.

"If it ain't the gangster Rishon," laughed Malik. "What's good, cat? I hear your bitch-ass was hiding under the bed. It figures," said Malik. Smiling and turning to Elaine, he asked, "Hey baby, are you alright, sweetheart?"

Elaine jumped at the chance to come out of this not only unharmed, but ahead of the game. She started her act, doing what she did best. Elaine jumped up and ran into Malik's arms and started weeping.

"Oh, baby, I'm so glad to see you. I wanted to come home long ago, baby. But Rishon, he just wouldn't let me leave," said Elaine, looking into Malik's eyes. She wanted to see if he was buying her story. "Oh baby, I miss you so much. Please just get me out of here and take me home."

Big-O looked at Nes and AG. It was clear that they were not buying the act but remained silent and kept listening.

"Okay boo, you're safe now. I miss you so much," said Malik kissing his wife.

She passionately returned his kiss. Rishon looked on in disbelief before finally opening his mouth.

"You bitch! That's some grimy shit. You came here on your own. I ain't surprised at this slick shit you pulling. My sister tried to warn me about trying to turn a ho' into a damn housewife," said Rishon. There was anger and shame mixed in with his drunken high. He let it all out when he continued. "Yo Malik, you can keep that grimy ho'. When you kiss her, tell me if you can taste my cum in your mouth, nigga. Ha, ha, ha…"

Malik lost his mind. He walked over to the couch and put six shots in Rishon's head. Then he spat a gobble of saliva on the bloody body. Malik grabbed Elaine's hand and walked her out of the apartment and down into the courtyard.

"Malik, what you want us to do with the rest of these people that's still hiding in their apartments?" asked AG, coming down the stairs.

"It's all over. Let them burn, baby. I really don't care. I got what I came for," said Malik, looking at Elaine.

Nes, Big-O and AG stood in the courtyard. They saw residents running up and down grabbing their children and valuables. Finally they piled out of the burning building in tears. They watched the building slowly going up in flames.

In the distance, the sound of fire engines and police sirens made them look at each other before Big-O broke the silence.

"Yo, man, this mess was some real bullshit. We lost our boy and some good men over what, a stripper? I hope that nigga is happy now. He got his. Everyone else lost tonight, except that selfish-ass Malik."

Chapter 10

"Here's to Hill and all the other fallen soldiers."

Big-O, Nes and A.G. lifted their glasses, toasting their dead friends. It was one year to the day since the siege on Stevenson Commons. The crew had come together to remember their boys. They were holding a remembrance vigil in the back room at a Harlem Bar and Grill, awaiting Malik's arrival.

"Baby, where's my blue gators?" asked Malik while getting dressed to meet up with his boys.

Elaine was breastfeeding her three-month-old baby. Shortly after Malik and Elaine came home after the Bronx ordeal, she discovered that she was pregnant. Malik couldn't have been happier at first, but shortly after the baby was born Elaine became cold and indifferent. She hardly spoke to Malik and he was getting annoyed with her newfound attitude.

"You hear me Elaine? Where my gators at…?"

"How the hell should I know? Can't you see that I'm feeding my baby?"

Malik went to the closet to get a shirt. The shirt he wanted to wear was wrinkled and he looked at Elaine.

"Didn't I ask you to iron this shirt for me? Damn, you don't cook, clean, you don't do shit but sit on your ass all day. And when I ask for one little favor I can't even get that. Your ass is so useless," said Malik, walking to the couch to see his son.

He reached out to take him and Elaine pulled the baby away saying, "Can't you see that I'm feeding him? Don't you have somewhere to go?"

"I can't believe I went to war over a fucking useless bitch like you," said Malik.

He was feeling totally disrespected with the abuse metered out by his wife and let Elaine have it. Before Malik could walk away, Elaine shot back her own venomous remark.

"Nigga, no one told you to come after me. I was fine where I was at. I ain't your domestic help. So if that's what you expected when you married me, then you buggin'. I'm not the one," said Elaine, looking at Malik with hatred in her eyes then she threw the final blow. "Shit, Rishon never asked me to cook and clean. He was just happy hitting this bomb ass puss…"

She didn't get a chance to finish. Malik punched Elaine

straight in the mouth. She toppled to the floor and the baby fell harmlessly on the couch. Malik picked up his son and took him to his room, placing him in the crib. He returned to the living room and saw Elaine standing there holding her jaw. When she felt in her mouth and realized that several of her teeth were missing, Elaine flipped. Jumping on Malik, she punched him and kicked him, swinging like a mad woman.

Malik's rage was blinded by Elaine's verbal and emotional abuse since his son's birth. He started fighting Elaine as if she was a man, punching her repeatedly, and stomping her when she was down on the ground. Elaine was a bloody mess after the fisticuffs was over. She had a broken nose, busted lips, one eye was closed shut, and she had lost three teeth. Her trademark beauty was shattered.

Malik calmly got dressed and started walking to the door after beating his wife half to death. Before he could leave, Elaine lying on the living room floor slurred out her last comment to her husband.

"You're gonna pay for this, nigga. Believe that," snarled Elaine in an acid-laced tone.

Malik turned around and smiled before closing the door. He walked away feeling confident.

"Where is Malik? Everyone's getting ready to leave. Just like him to show up late even to honor his boy. That selfish muthafucka!" said AG with contempt.

AG never really forgave Malik for getting them involved in the Stevenson Commons drama, and he secretly blamed Malik for Hill's death.

"He'll be here, man. Plus this is really a time for us to look back and remember Hill and our boys who are not here with us. These freeloaders are just here for food and liquor, let 'em breakout," argued Nes, bidding goodbye to chicks he knew.

Later they sat at a table and a waitress came over with a cordless phone.

"There's a call for you AG. It's a woman, but she don't wanna give her name."

"Probably one of your bitches, pimp," teased Big-O, pouring another drink.

"Hello, yeah, this is AG. Who is... Oh, what's up? Malik ain't here. I'll..." said AG followed by a long silence.

AG listened to the conversation coming from the caller. His expression slowly started to change. His boys all noticed and started to get curious. AG continued listening for a few more minutes before saying, "Yeah, okay, good looking. I kinda always figured that was the real, but thanks for confirming it for me. Peace."

Hanging up the phone, AG spun around and was furious. "Well, my brothers, it's like I figured."

"Like you figured? What you talking about, A?" questioned Nes.

"Your boy set us up from the word go, that's what's up. That was Elaine on the phone. She was never kidnapped. She went to Rishon on her own. All that shit about bringing her back from a kidnapping and the back door being broken into was bullshit. That bastard played us and caused us to go to war to bring back a ho' who didn't even want to be rescued."

They all sat stunned, listening to AG. Hearing all what he had to say Big-O rubbed his bald head before answering.

"Hold up. You tellin' me that we risked our lives and brothers lost their lives, over some jealousy bullshit and lies. Please tell me that's not what you saying, AG?"

"That's exactly what he's saying, Big-O. It's funny but I think we all had our suspicions from the jump. Yeah, that nigga, Malik, played us good and we lost our boy Hill because of it," said Nes, pausing to get his thoughts together.

"I don't know what y'all thinking, but I know what I'm thinking," said a now angry AG.

The men sat discussing and arguing the importance of the new information. They started their conversation undecided, but as the liquor and their tempers kept flowing they came to a unanimous but painful decision.

"Sorry I'm late cats. I had to take care of some shit at home. Where's my drink?" asked Malik, walking in and strolling to the bar.

"What you drinking, playa?" asked Nes from behind the bar.

"This cat is down for that Hen dog. Let's get this party started right," laughed Malik.

"Started, brother this shit started hours ago. But it's definitely about to be over. Yo Malik, we just got the strangest phone call from a friend. And what's funny is the call came on the anniversary of Hill's death," said AG to Malik, moving closer to him.

"What's so funny about a call tonight?" asked Malik, feeling a little jittery without fully understanding the reason.

"It's funny because Elaine shed some light as to what the beef at Stevenson Commons last year was really about," said AG.

Malik gulped his drink and looked at Big-O then heard the bolt to the back door being locked. He looked at Nes and AG. They both had him surrounded and their intentions were clear. Malik took another swig, closing his eyes and said, "Damn, I guess I fucked up.

Elaine called her girlfriend who took her to the emergency room at Westchester Community Hospital. She had several injuries but none were life threatening, because of internal bleeding, Elaine remained in the hospital for three days under doctor's observation.

She went home to pack her bags, and leave Malik when she was finally released from the hospital. Elaine was a street-smart hustler, and was not leaving empty-handed. She cleaned out Malik's safe and took all his money and jewelry then packed her own personal belongings. Elaine went to her son's room and packed his clothes. Her son had been staying at her aunt's house while she was in the hospital. She picked him up on her way home.

"Baby, we're gonna start a new life, just me and you. I love you, and I promise to always love and cherish you no matter what" said Elaine, kissing her baby and picking him up. "Before we leave town, I want you to meet somebody."

Elaine left the house Malik bought her for the last time. She drove with her baby to a new but uncertain life.

"Here we are. Before we left, I needed you to meet your real father. Say hello to your daddy."

Elaine looked at the headstone and said, "This is your baby boy. I just wanted you to see him before we left." Elaine paused for a moment, wiping her eyes then said, "Say goodbye daddy."

Elaine started to walk away from the gravesite that she and her baby visited. She headed out of the cemetery and bundled up her baby boy, kissing him softly on the cheek. "You look so much like your handsome father. I love you so much. Come on, Heckie, let's go."

THE END

About the author

The author Stephen Hewett, a forty-four year old native New Yorker of Jamaican decent was raised in the Bronx. Early years found Hewett spending most of his childhood in Kingston with his grandmother. During his adolescent years, Hewett attended Catholic schools in NY, and did very well in his academic studies. The eighties brought the appeal of street life to many of his peers. Stephen Hewett was no exception. He started hustlin' in mid-town Manhattan after high school. Although Hewett attended college and raised a family, his illegal activities caused him several years of incarceration and hardships.

You'll never take me alive copper...

Well they did take me alive, and they took away my freedom, my loot and many valuable years with my family. They say everything happens for a reason, I truly believe that the reason I went to prison besides my obvious criminal behavior, was so I could and should start writing. Prisoners choose to do their time in many different ways. They cope with the stressful everyday drama by engaging in various outlets. Some prisoners take out their frustrations in the gym, others play the yard all day. You have those who take to the law books to work on their appeals. You even have the less enthusiastic prisoners who watch BET or the stories all day. Although I spent many years getting my body in shape, I also spent the same amount of time getting my literary works in shape. With books, poems and greeting cards in the stash, I emerged from the federal prison system to reclaim my freedom and family. I am ready to start hustling again, but this time I will hustle a safer and long term product, my mind and my talent to write…

Stephen Hewett

Contact the author at

www.streetlitreview.com and Shewett41@yahoo.com

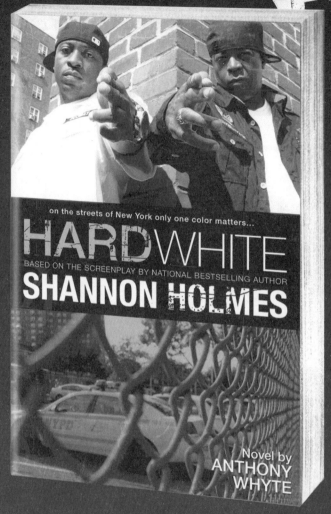

Hard White: On the street of New York only on color matters
Novel By Anthony Whyte Based on the screenplay by Shannon Holmes

The streets are pitch black...A different shade of darkness has drifted to the North Bronx neighborhood known as Edenwald. Sleepless nights, there is no escaping dishonesty, disrespect, suspicion, ignorance, hostility, treachery, violence, karma... Hard White metered out to the residents. Two, Melquan and Precious have big dreams but must overcome much in order to manifest theirs. Hard White the novel is a story of triumph and tribulations of two people's journey to make it despite the odds. Nail biting drama you won't ever forget...Once you pick it up you can't put it down. Deftly written by Anthony Whyte based on the screenplay by Shannon Holmes, the story comes at you fast, furiously offering an insight to what it takes to get off the streets. It shows a woman's unWlimited love for her man. Precious is a rider and will do it all again for her man, Melquan... His love for the street must be bloodily severed. Her love for him will melt the coldest heart...Together their lives hang precariously over the crucible of Hard White. Read the novel and see why they make the perfect couple.

$14.95 // 9780982541531

NATIONAL BESTSELLING AUTHOR

ANTHONY WHYTE

STREET CHIĆ

A NOVEL

Street Chic
By Anthony Whyte

A new case comes across the desk of detective Sheryl Street, from the Dade county larceny squad in Miami. Pursuing the investigation she discovers that it threatens to unfold some details of her life she thought was left buried in the Washington Heights area of New York City. Her duties as detective pits her against a family that had emotionally destabilized her. Street ran away from a world she wanted nothing to do with. The murder of a friend brings her back as law and order. Surely as night time follows daylight, Street's forced into a resolve she cannot walk away from. Loyalty is tested when a deadly choice has to be made. When you read this dark and twisted novel you'll find out if allegiance to her family wins Street over. A most interesting moral conundrum exists in the dramatic t i n that is Street Chic.

WHen LOVE TURns TO HaTe

A NOVEL BY
SHARRON DOYLE

When Love Turns To Hate
By Sharron Doylee

Petie is back regulating from down south. He rides with a new ruthless partner, and they're all about making fast money. The partners mercilessly go after a shady associate who is caught in an FBI sting and threatens their road to riches. Petie and his two sons have grown apart. Renee, their mother, has to make a big decision when one of her sons wild-out. Desperately, she tries to keep her world from crumbling while holding onto what's left of her family. Venus fights for life after suffering a brutal physical attack. Share goes to great lengths to make sure her best friend's attacker stays ruined forever. Crazy entertaining and teeming with betrayal, corruption, and murder, When Love Turns To Hate is mixed with romance gone awry. The drama will leave you panting for more....

$14.95 // 9780982541517

SMUT central
By Brandon McCalla

Markus Johnson, so mysterious he barely knows who he is. An infant left at the doorstep of an orphanage. After fleeing his refuge, he was taken in by a couple with a perverse appetite for sexual indiscretions, only to become a star in the porn industry... Dr. Nancy Adler, a shrink who gained a peculiar patient, unlike any she has ever encountered. A young African American man who faints upon sight of a woman he has never met, having flashbacks of a past he never knew existed. A past that contradicts the few things he knows about himself... Sex and lust tangled in a web so disgustingly tantalizing and demented. Something evil, something demonic... Something beyond the far reaches of a porn stars mind, peculiar to a well established shrink, leaving an old NYPD detective on the verge of solving a case that has been a dead end for years... all triggered by desires for a mysterious woman...

$14.95 // 9780982541586

Dead And Stinkin'
By Stephen Hewett

Stephen Hewett Collection brings you love as crime. Timeless folklores of adventure, heroes and heroines suffering for love. Can deep unconditional love overcome any obstacles? What is ghetto love? One time loyal friends turned merciless enemies. Humorous and powerful Dead and Stinkin' is tragic and twisted folktales from author Stephen Hewett. The Stephen Hewett Collection comes alive with 3 intensely gripping short stories of undying love, coupled with modern day lies, deceit and treachery.

$14.95 // 9780982541555

Power of the P
By James Hendricks

Erotica at its gritty best, Power of the P is the seductive story of an entrepreneur who wields his powerful status in unimaginable — and sometimes unethical — ways. This exotic ride through the underworld of sex and prostitution in the hood explores how sex is leveraged to gain advantage over friends and rivals alike, and how sometimes the white collar world and the streets aren't as different as we thought they were.

$14.95 // 9780982541579

America's Soul
By Erick S Gray

Soul has just finished his 18-month sentence for a parole violation. Still in love with his son's mother, America, he wants nothing more than for them to become a family and move on from his past. But while Soul was in prison, America's music career started blowing up and she became entangled in a rocky relationship with a new man, Kendall. Kendall is determined to keep his woman by his side, and America finds herself caught in a tug of war between the two men. Soul turns his attention to battling the street life that landed him in jail — setting up a drug program to rid the community of its tortuous meth problem — but will Soul's efforts cross his former best friend, the murderous drug kingpin Omega?

$14.95 // 9780982541548

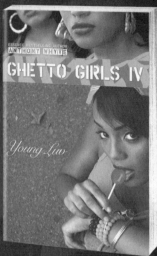

GHETTO GIRLS I

Young Luv

ESSENCE BESTSELLING AUTH
ANTHONY WHYT

ESSENCE BESTSELLING AUTHOR
ANTHONY WHYTE

GHETTO GIRLS IV

Young Luv

Ghetto Girls IV Young Luv
$14.95 // 9780979281662

Ghetto Girls
$14.95 // 0975945319

Ghetto Girls Too
$14.95 // 0975945300

Ghetto Girls 3 Soo H
$14.95 // 0975945351

THE BEST OF THE STREET CHRONICLES TODAY, THE **GHETTO GIRLS SERIES** IS A
WONDERFULLY HYPNOTIC ADVENTURE THAT DELVES INTO THE CONVOLUTED MINDS
OF CRIMINALS AND THE DARK WORLD OF POLICE CORRUPTION. YET, THERE IS
SOMETHING THRILLING AND SURPRISINGLY TENDER ABOUT THIS ONGOING
YOUNG-ADULT SAGA FILLED WITH MAD FLAVA.

Love and a Gangsta
author // **ERICK S GRAY**

This explosive sequel to **Crave All Lose All**. Soul and America
were together ten years 'til Soul's incarceration for drugs.
Faithfully, she waited four years for his return. Once home they
find life ain't so easy anymore. America believes in holding her
man down and expects Soul to be as committed. His lust for
fast money rears its ugly head at the same time America's mus
career takes off. From shootouts, to hustling and thugging life,
Soul and his man, Omega, have done it. Omega is on the
come-up in the drug-game of South Jamaica, Queens. Using
ties to a Mexican drug cartel, Omega has Queens in his grip. His
older brother, Rahmel, was Soul's cellmate in an upstate prison
Rahmel, a man of God, tries to counsel Soul. Omega introduces
New York to crystal meth. Misery loves company and on the roa
to the riches and spoils of the game, Omega wants the only ma
he can trust, Soul, with him. Love between Soul and America is
tested by an unforgivable greed that leads quickly to deception
and murder.

$14.95 // 9780979281648

A POWERFUL UNFORGIVING STORY
CREATED BY HIP HOP LITERATURE'S BESTSELLING AUTHORS

THIS THREE-VOLUME KILLER STORY FEATURING FOREWORDS FROM
SHANNON HOLMES, K'WAN & **TREASURE BLUE**

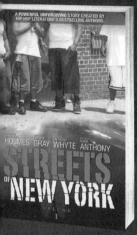
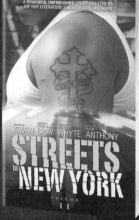
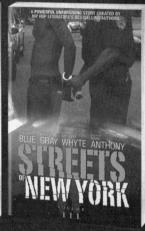

reets of New York vol. 1 | Streets of New York vol. 2 | Streets of New York vol. 3
4.95 // 9780979281679 | $14.95 // 9780979281662 | $14.95 // 9780979281662

AN EXCITING, ENCHANTING... A FUNNY, THRILLING AND EXHILARATING
RIDE THROUGH THE ROUGH NEIGHBORHOODS OF THE GRITTY CITY. THE MOST FUN YOU
CAN LEGALLY HAVE WITHOUT ACTUALLY LIVING ON THE STREETS OF NEW YORK. READ
THE STORY FROM HIP HOP LITERATURE TOP AUTHORS:

ERICK S. GRAY, MARK ANTHONY & ANTHONY WHYTE

Lipstick Diaries Part 2
A Provocative Look into the Female Perspective
Foreword by **WAHIDA CLARK**

Lipstick Diaries II is the second coming together of some of the most
unique, talented female writers of Hip Hop Literature. Featuring a
feast of short stories from today's top authors. **Genieva Borne, Camo,
Endy, Brooke Green, Kineisha Gayle, the queen of hip hop lit; Carolyn
McGill, Vanessa Martir, Princess Madison, Keisha Seignious**, and a
blistering foreword served up by the queen of thug love; Ms. **Wahida
Clark**. Lipstick Diaries II pulls no punches, there are no bars hold
leaves no metaphor unturned. The anthology delivers a knockout with
stories of pain and passion, love and virtue, profit and gain, ... all told
with flair from the women's perspective. Lipstick Diaries II is a
must-read for all.

$14.95 // 9780979281655

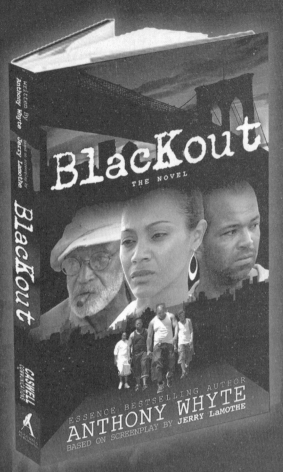

The lights went out
and the
mayhem began.

It's gritty in the city but hotter in Brooklyn where a small community in east Flatbush must come to grips with its greatest threat, self-destruction. August 14 and 15, 2003, the eastern section of the United States is crippled by a major shortage of electrical power, the worst in US history. Blackout, the spellbinding novel is based on the epic motion picture, directed by Jerry Lamothe. A thoroughly riveting story with delectable details of families caught in a harsh 48 hours of random violent acts, exploding in deadly conflict. There's a message in everything... even the bullet. The author vividly places characters on the stage of life and like pieces on a chess-board, expertly moves them to a tumultuous end. Voila! Checkmate, a literary triumph. Blackout is a masterpiece. This heart-stopping, page-turning drama is moving fast. Blackout is destined to become an American classic.

BASED ON SCREENPLAY BY **JERRY LaMOTHE**

Inspired by true events

US $14.95 CAN $20.95
ISBN 978-0-9820653-0-3

CASWELL
COMMUNICATION